His Chosen Bride

Sherry Gloag

The Gasquet Princes
book two

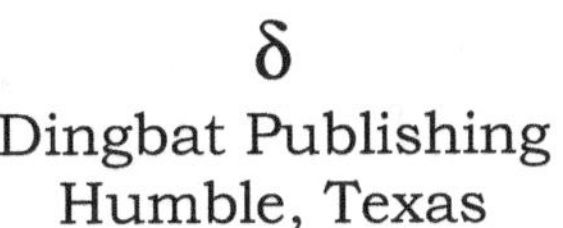

δ

Dingbat Publishing
Humble, Texas

One

Henri Pierre Gasquet hesitated before knocking on his father's office door. They'd shared breakfast together less than an hour ago and talked over many things, including Henri's killer schedule for the next several months. The king had given no indication of the need for a formal meeting at that time, and so his father's missive, left on his desk by his secretary, had surprised him. With a fatalistic shrug, Henri knocked, waited a second, then turned the handle and entered the room.

"You wanted to see me?" He waited for his father to indicate he should sit before dropping into the chair in front of the king's desk.

"I have not been unaware of the burden you have carried since my heart attack a year ago."

Shocked, Henri watched as the king flipped through the pages of his diary and sighed before stopping at today's entries. He pointed to the itemised list of appointments and cast a disappointed stare in Henri's direction before turning it round for Henri to read.

Who'd passed his official diary to his father?

"Combining your own commitments with those you took over while I recuperated would have felled a lesser man." The king's voice hardened.

Feeling the heat burn his cheeks, Henri shifted in his chair. The past twelve months had been tough, and for the last six, his advisors had almost competed with each other in counselling him to slow down unless he wanted to occupy his father's hospital bed.

"I am also aware you have ignored all advice to cut back. So I am decreeing that as of this moment, you are on an indeterminate leave of absence."

"What!" Shock propelled Henri from his chair, and anxiety chased him round the room while he tried to remarshall his scattered thoughts. "I don't have time to take leave of any kind," he snapped. "This morning I am presiding over the ceremony to lay the new foundations for the bridge that will connect the west of our country more directly with the east." He tunneled his fingers through his hair. "This afternoon, I have a meeting with the backers about the funds for Melanie's riding school for the disabled, and this evening I am giving a speech to the leaders of our financial sector."

He planted his knuckles on his father's desk and leaned forward. "I can't just take off and leave them all in the lurch." He pushed away. "It is ridiculous for you or anyone else to expect me to walk away from my duties. Who would take my place?" he challenged, knowing every project mentioned needed his influence and prestige to press the developments forward.

"I will."

His father's bald statement rocked Henri back on his heels. "You?"

"It is a year since my heart attack," the king said again, "and for the most part I have accepted the dictates of my doctors and advisors, and am now taking a leaf out of my son's book before my heir drops dead from physical and emotional exhaustion."

With a snap, the king closed Henri's diary and leaned back in his chair. Instead of pushing it towards him, the king slipped the diary into one of the desk drawers, his gaze still focused on his son.

"So you, my son, are on leave until I say otherwise."

Feeling like a recalcitrant four-year-old, Henri recognised that tone of voice now and sighed. A lenient parent in most things, his father at times used a tone that brooked no argument. This was one of those times, Henri acknowledged.

"What am I supposed to do?" For the life of him, he failed to conceal his sarcasm. "Twiddle my thumbs? And for how long?"

"Until I say otherwise."

A beam of sunlight transformed the king's thatch of grey hair to silver. His eyes conveyed simultaneous messages of understanding and determination. He rose and rounded his desk. Resting his hand on Henri's shoulder, the king softened his tone. "Get away, right away, and relax. Do you suppose I've found it easy to watch you running yourself into the ground in your efforts to combine your schedule with mine? And now—? Now," he paused, waiting for a reaction that Henri swallowed before continuing. "Now it is time for me to take up the reins again.

"The plane is waiting to take you to Scotland. Melanie and Liam hope you will remain with them for a couple of months at least, until you are fully rested.

"If the thought of staying beyond Christmas stifles you, Liam did suggest that if you could not tolerate remaining in one place that long, you take a leaf out of his book and travel the world for a few months.

"It's not as if we face the same security problems the insurgents caused for your brother and Melanie, so if that is what you want to do—" The king's face crinkled into genuine mirth. "I promise you, your bodyguards are all well known to you."

With a *harrumph,* Henri failed to hide his amusement. Liam's marriage to his protector was a standing family joke now.

"I gather you have talked with Liam and Melanie, and no doubt held a family conference. Therefore I will go, as it seems I have no choice in the matter. But I'll remind you, unlike my brother, I am prepared to marry a bride of your choice. It worked for you and Mother. And I see no reason why, if my proposed bride is chosen with care, I cannot emulate your example."

Henri wondered whether he imagined the shudder of distaste that flipped across his father's face, it was gone so quickly.

"Your transport awaits you," was all his father said before wrapping him in a bear hug. "Go talk to your mother before you leave."

Beyond her front door the first snow of winter fell, soft as stealth, and it covered the driveway. Inside, silence filled the room while she sat staring at the fire.

"Can you see the pictures in the flames?" The soft Scottish burr of her late mother's voice crossed the barrier of time as clearly as if she stood next to Monica.

She'd been five the first time her mother asked the question. Five, and eager to experience a new adventure. For hours she'd sat in front of the fire, its orange flames curling 'round the logs her father cut and hauled in each morning. At first she'd pretended to herself and her mother she'd seen all sorts of things. The pony she wished for, peering over the stable door that didn't exist, the baby brother who arrived two years later, and the puppy her best friend Lillian received. She even imagined she saw the letters written in the flames of the name Lillian chose for her new friend.

"You'll never guess what I just got!" Lillian had bounced into the school playground the following day, her face glowing with excitement.

"A puppy?" Until she heard the words, saw her breath mist in the cold playground air, she'd not realised she'd spoken aloud.

Deflated, Lillian glowered at her. "How'd you know that?" Then she'd beamed her usual sunny smile. "I s'pose my mom told you and made you promise not to tell."

Not quite sure why, Monica remained silent, but assumed perhaps that was how she knew.

When Lillian asked her to guess the puppy's name, Monica thought she'd sealed her lips and hoped that her best friend had not heard her say *Jasper.*

"Jasper!" Lillian squealed while jumping up and down on the spot and clapping her hands together.

A frisson of trepidation had skittered up Monica's spine. How had she known? Had her friend mentioned a liking for the name? If so, she couldn't remember. Her fear grew when later that evening she recounted the incident to her mother and was met by a concerned silence.

Her mother's smile, usually so open and encouraging, faltered and slipped away altogether. Her smoky blue eyes, usually filled with love and laughter, turned chilly. Her voice when she answered was the most frightening of all.

"Don't tell lies, Monica," she'd snapped. Instead

of the usual nighttime hug, her mother stepped back from the bed, ordered Monica to say her prayers twice and to include a request for forgiveness for telling lies, before halting in the doorway, her hand on the knob. "And if this is the result of sitting staring at the fire so much, I suggest you find something more constructive to do with your time."

The slamming of the bedroom door punctuated her mother's words.

Miserable, confused, and suddenly tired beyond sleeping, she'd pulled the covers over her head and cried into her pillow throughout the night.

In the morning, Monica decided her mother's smile could freeze the fires of hell. Her jittery stomach refused to accept the breakfast placed in front of her and she left for school feeling sick, tired, and hungry all at once.

When Lillian ran up to her, Monica sighed with relief; at least she had her friend. And then she noticed Lillian's stony-faced glare.

"My mom said she never told you about the puppy, so how did you know, and how did you guess the correct name?"

To Monica, it seemed everyone in the playground stopped and waited for her answer. Isolation, heavy and penetrating, weighed down on her shoulders. What could she say? She didn't know, so she took the easy way out and simply shrugged.

In that moment everything changed.

Her school life changed.

When she approached, conversations stopped. Instead of sharing camaraderie, her former school friends ignored her.

She learned to stand alone.

At home her parents walked round her as though she'd caught the plague. There too, she learned to stand alone. Only her brother, Billy, penetrated the barrier of self-preservation she erected.

And now?

Now, nearly twenty years later, she sat in front of her hearth, her hands cradled round her knees, and watched some of the earliest images she could remember of her mother playing with her in the snow, before she'd encouraged her daughter to seek pictures in the flames.

All water under the bridge, she thought, and let her memories fast forward to her mother's final year.

For the six months before she'd died, her mother accepted her daughter's offer of healing to alleviate the pain.

During those months they talked. Really talked.

"I'm sorry." Her mother's frail voice drew Monica's attention as she sat at the hospital bedside.

"Sorry?" Bewildered, she'd searched for explanations and come up empty. Her parents had dished out edicts as she'd grown up, and on the few occasions when she returned home after escaping at sixteen, she was usually met with disapproval.

"Your grandmother had the gift," her mother started. "Knowing you could inherit her abilities, your father threatened to walk away from us if you developed it. I promised him if he stayed I wouldn't let you progress with your gift."

No wonder her father treated her like a pariah, Monica thought as she struggled to marshal her thoughts.

And the irony?

He'd left anyway. Maybe not for ten years, but he'd left her mother for a newer model. And she'd been shattered.

Filled with an unexplained guilt about the breakup, Monica took off a few months later.

At first she'd buried the perplexing experiences

that bombarded her. Later, when new friends discovered her gift, they'd come to her for help and advice. Finally, after some hefty pleading, she'd succumbed and let the feelings and 'knowing' in.

The sense of isolation, both inner and outer, eased, and in time disappeared. She felt complete, if not quite comfortable with circumstances. And now her mother informed her it was genetically inherited.

The relationship between them grew closer, and finally Monica recognised that barely remembered loving glow in her mother's eyes.

"Yes, I remember when you encouraged me to look for pictures in the fire," Monica replied, her words echoing in the silence around her.

"Never stop." Her mother's voice, as loud as her own, filled Monica's mind. "Never stop watching. Never stop dreaming." It faltered, dropped. "Fire, like love, can burn or warm. Never let the fire within you go out."

A log in the grate shifted, sending sparks soaring up the chimney. The silence around her shimmered and settled, and a warmth like a scarf wrapped around Monica's heart.

She lost track of time until the flames caught her attention once more. They flickered from orange to gold, to silver, to white.

A flurry of snowflakes masked the flames, and for a second Monica watched the most beautiful, pristine snow-scene she'd ever seen. Her lips curved in longing. How she'd love to get a toboggan and slide down that slope. She knew where it was, and had done just that many times in her childhood, first with her parents and then, in a clandestine manner, with her brother. Sneaking an old tin tray from the back of her mother's walk-in pantry, she'd then grabbed Billy's hand, and they'd rushed out the back gate, heading for the lakeside track that led up into the hills.

Darkness, dense and thick with grief, dropped over the scene. Startled and disconcerted by the strength of emotion emanating from the vision, Monica shifted to her knees, ready to stand, when a voice, a deep male voice sharp with fear, called out her name.

"Monica!"

She knew she'd never heard the voice before, and yet — it was as familiar to her as the image she saw in her mirror each morning.

"Help me, Monica."

Desperate for more clues, she searched the darkness within the flames until it sputtered and faded. With a curse, she jumped up and ran for the phone. With her outstretched hand hovering over it, she halted and let her hand drop to her side once more. What could she say? What would the police or rescue team think if she called them and told them she'd seen a vision of a man in distress?

They'd laugh in her face and classify her as a lunatic. Well, maybe not. It wouldn't be the first time she'd contacted them with positive information; but something — an instinctive gut reaction — told her what she'd seen this time hadn't happened yet.

Who could she call? Who would understand? And then she laughed at her own stupidity. Melanie. Of course, her best friend Melanie would get it, would understand and offer sound counsel. She picked up the phone, dialled, and waited.

Two

December 24

"Tell me about your favourite Christmas." Melanie settled into her chair and watched the two brothers stare at each other as if they'd been pole-axed. In the background, the Christmas tree lights twinkled on the ten-foot Scots pine standing in the corner of the room. "Surely you celebrated Christmas at the palace?" Concern for the royal siblings pushed her back in her chair.

"Well." Liam hesitated, gaped at her, cleared his throat, and sat on the arm of her chair. Henri, his elder brother and the heir to the throne of a tiny European country bordering Switzerland, cast a puzzled glance at both of them.

"We grew up with the knowledge that Christmas belonged to our people." Henri started slowly and, when Liam nodded, settled on the other arm of Melanie's chair. "It wasn't like here in Britain where your Royals do a Christmas speech to the nation while holidaying in the wilds of Norfolk. We were physically on display."

"What! All day, all of you?" In sitting up, Melanie nearly sent both brothers flying. "Surely you had some family time together away from the media spotlight?"

The following silence pounded in her head as she imagined the royal siblings on a palace balcony. One like those she'd dreamed about as a child. She couldn't say her own Christmases had been full of joy, but those of the Gasquets carried a different kind of emotional deprivation. She knew, from years of close official association with the king and his queen, they were good, loving parents; so why had they allowed their country to take precedence over their children's needs on that one special day of the year?

"I thought mine were bad," she muttered and started when Henri broke through her thoughts.

"What do you mean?" he asked.

Before his wife could reply Liam interrupted, knowing just the thought of her treatment as a child could reduce Melanie to tears in a second. "Fists for kisses," he stated flatly, and with a meaningful glance at his brother changed the subject. "Do you remember that year when, after we came in from the first balcony appearance, we ran off and hid?"

Henri's laughter eased the tension and to Melanie's relief, redirected his thoughts to the ensuing mayhem. "They turned the whole palace upside down and involved everyone in the search.

"Of course, at that time we were too young to know or appreciate anything about the security threats from the insurgents. To us it was just a bid for freedom from the monotony of routine on a day when we knew from the television that other people had a really joyful time. Our parents even called in the air force to join the search."

Melanie almost laughed aloud when Henri slanted a rueful grin in her direction.

"And all this time, you were where?"

"Where do you think four boys up to no good would go in a palace?"

"You didn't!" She remembered the locked door Liam pointed out to her on her first visit to the palace as his wife.

"The dungeons," he said.

"We did!" Liam joined in with his brother's recollections.

"Weren't you frightened? Wasn't it dark and damp down there?" When they shook their heads, she added, "I thought all dungeons were dark and damp."

"No. Not at all," Henri said. "We often played down there and had stored a collection of candles, torches, packets of biscuits, and—" He paused before continuing in a conspiratorial tone. "—we found some old chairs that had been junked at some time and a rickety old table from one of the other rooms."

"We convinced ourselves they came from one of the warden's quarters," Liam added with glee. "When we went back upstairs, the whole place was in uproar. We were grounded for a week and the dungeons were locked up after that."

The front doorbell interrupted any further reminiscences.

"That will be Monica." Liam rose and departed to admit their visitor.

"Monica?"

Caution warred with anticipation as Henri's mind raced back to an image of the woman who'd unknowingly almost brought him to his knees the first time he'd seen her: The shuffling of the congregation — or to be more exact, the one thousand guests invited to his youngest brother's affirmation of his marriage vows to his bride, Melanie Babcott — mingled with the snippets of quiet conversations throughout the cathedral when the hairs on the back of his neck tingled. He didn't need the blast of organ music to inform him the ceremony had begun. Expecting to see his sister-in-law coming down the aisle, he saw a sprite of a woman dressed in a full-length midnight-blue chiffon gown with almost-there straps on her slender shoulders. The face of an angel, caught as it was in a shaft of sunlight beaming down through the plain thirteenth-century glass high above the congregation.

The memory of his fear of suffering a heart attack when his heart started racing resurfaced, as well as how his knees almost buckled beneath him. Liam's hand clutching his arm, Henri remembered, had brought him back to reality.

"You're not matchmaking, are you?" he had demanded. His heart had pounded so hard it threatened to jump out of his chest.

And now with only a few seconds' warning, he knew she'd disturb him all over again...

He remembered when they'd danced together. Once. The obligatory best-man-and-bridesmaid dance, and every night since then, she came to him in his dreams and every night he reached out for her, could swear he smelled her light flowery scent, feel the touch of her hand as it had rested against his chest. And every morning he woke, frustrated, cold and wanting.

He'd worked his socks off to try and banish her from his mind and almost succeeded, and now — now he'd have to start all over again.

Or would he?

The king had demanded he take a break. Get some rest. Have some fun. Well, perhaps he could have some fun with the witch who'd mesmerised him. A holiday flirtation. Why not? He pinned his sister-in-law with a glare. "I hope you are not matchmaking," he said, grimly satisfied when he disconcerted her with his abruptness.

"Monica is my friend and partner in the riding business," she said primly, before adding firmly, "and I would never try to set her up with an unwanted date. She's alone this Christmas and agreed to join us long before we knew whether you were visiting us, too."

He nodded acceptance at her challenge, looked up when his brother re-entered the room, and fought to control his racing heart when he studied the newcomer. How in all the maelstrom of his eviction from his job and his home had he not considered the possibility — no, *probability* — of seeing Monica Latimer again?

Well, now he'd exorcise her influence over him in the most primitive way possible between a man and a woman. Perhaps this enforced holiday would be more fun than anticipated.

He'd heard the phrase 'hair like spun gold,' and suddenly understood why some unknown man, one he'd formerly rubbished as 'witless,' had waxed lyrical. Hers fell in soft waves to her shoulders before turning inward. Her eyes reminded him of the emeralds in the royal vault back home. Large, round, and instead of reflecting colour, hers held a myriad of emotions.

Skin like alabaster...

No!

He shook his thoughts clear; her skin was rosy from the cold breeze outside, her lips held the ghost of a smile tinged with accusation — and the smile was directed, he saw, at his sister-in-law.

She rose, dashed across the room, and threw her arms around her friend.

"It's not what you think," Melanie assured her friend in gentle tones. "Remember we told you about trying to persuade Henri to join us this year?"

The girl nodded.

Well, hardly a girl, Henri admitted as his tongue slid round inside his suddenly parched mouth.

"Well," Melanie continued, "it was your suggestion that we appeal to the king to tip the balance and get Henri to join us for Christmas—"

"What?" Henri's eyes narrowed. This slip of a chit had schemed with Liam and Melanie to turn his life upside down? Anger and indignation warred with the desire raging through him, shooting any thought of immersing himself in a holiday flirtation out the window.

Straightening his shoulders, his lips thinning, he bowed, and said in his most regal tone, "So I owe the total disruption of my life to you, do I? It's always good to know your enemies."

He ignored the shocked gasps from his family and kept his gaze fixed on the woman. Well, he thought grimly, he'd go to great lengths to assure her that she was quite safe from him.

January 10

The simplicity of Christmas at the farm had appealed to Henri. The joy of seeing it through the eyes of his three-month-old nephew, Jonathon, intrigued him, and brought a new magic and meaning to the day. Yes, they'd exchanged presents and stuffed themselves motionless with the awesome food Melanie prepared. It was, he knew, a Christmas that would ever remain as one of his most precious memories.

He'd expected to chafe at the lack of a filled schedule, had wondered what he'd do with himself during this enforced period of inactivity, and laughed at the absurdity.

True, for the first few days, the disruption of his life, coupled with the re-entry of Monica into his orbit, stoked both his fury and sense of disconnection. Used to a life of routine with every moment accounted for, it took several days to acclimatise to the rhythm of the farm.

The sight of his brother's joy filled him with an unknown sense of yearning he couldn't identify. Heck, why had he never questioned that his life was all mapped out for him, that one day he'd step into his father's shoes, marry the woman his parents chose for him, sire the required heir and a spare, and—

His steps faltered. His mind jittered. He reflected back over the last few weeks, since his arrival.

To begin with, he'd stuck close to Liam, not only to learn what the farm and Melanie's riding school for the physically challenged amounted to, but simply for the unaccustomed pleasure of having unlimited time to enjoy his company.

It didn't take Henri long to pick up Liam's eagerness to share, to explain his enthusiasm for his new life and his part in training the horses used to help disabled children. He supposed that at some time he'd heard of such things, but as he watched Melanie, and occasionally Monica, working with them, the riders' joy transmitted itself to him.

A new life opened up in front of him, one he could never embrace, but to which he knew he could escape occasionally, for long or short breaks, whenever he wanted to.

Several volunteers gave their time to the charity; but it was watching Monica working with the children that soothed his soul and taught him there was far more to life than the meetings, duty, and ceremonies he'd immersed himself in so far.

Clearly the children loved her. Loved her spontaneity when they demanded trying something beyond their ability. Sometimes she shrugged her shoulders with a laugh and said "Why not?" and let them face a newer, bigger challenge than she'd thought they could handle. Sometimes she stood firm and kept her charges to the pre-arranged program. And everyone knew she shared and reciprocated the children's emotion. It flowed around the arena when she worked, echoed in the children's laughter each time they achieved a new goal. An emotional hole he hadn't known existed opened up in his heart while he watched. Would the woman his parents chose for him have the same empathy with children as Monica? He clamped down on the question and went in search of his brother.

He began spending more and more time around the stables; and if, while helping with the usual outdoor chores and seeing to the animals' welfare, his gaze strayed to where Monica worked, he refused to acknowledge it beyond noting how she removed her glove to tuck her hair back behind her ear every time the wind whipped it 'round her face.

He denied the increased heartbeat that thrummed within his chest in time to a mantra he tried to ignore.

Liar, liar, liar.

He watched as, with graceful efficiency, Monica moved on from one task to the next. Her appearance of fragility was deceptive, Henri discovered, when he caught her hefting a hay bale, and he rushed over to take it from her.

"It's okay," she said. "I've got it."

Ignoring her protest, he grabbed the pitchfork carrying her bale and followed her instructions. "You shouldn't be lifting these." He indicated the floor-to-roof stack of bales.

"I've been doing this for many years, Henri, and just because you suddenly see me at work doesn't change my reality."

From the beginning she'd ignored his title, and to start with he'd assumed she did it to annoy. But he soon realised it was her way of according him the same sense of belonging and family she offered Liam. So he ignored the warmth surrounding his heart that her actions triggered.

Normally soft-spoken, the snap in her voice startled him to immobility for all of ten seconds before he snatched the pitchfork out of her hands.

She stood back while he hefted the bale onto the high stack against the wall, and stuffed her hands into her jeans pockets. Judging from the glittering anger in her eyes, he reckoned she'd done that to prevent her fists from connecting with his chin.

Not just anger burning in her eyes, he decided, but anger in her heart as well. Anger — and passion. He gave in to his need to touch. He reached out, skimmed a knuckle down her cheek, and let his hand drift 'round to the back of her neck. His thumb traced the racing pulse at the base of her throat. So the lady was not as cool as she'd have him believe.

"You'll have to blame my mother," he claimed unrepentantly. "She taught us a gentleman never stood back if he saw a woman in distress."

Her gurgle of laughter entranced him. "I was hardly in distress, Henri."

He expected her to retreat, and curled a lock of her hair round his finger when she didn't.

"Monica?"

The shout from the house startled them both into stepping back. Her eyes, Henri noticed, had gone from smoky to glittering in the space of a heartbeat.

"In the barn," she answered.

"The phone," Melanie said as she reached the barn door. "James, from Round Haven House; he didn't tell me what he wanted, but I imagine it's about the Valentine's Day dance."

He gaped when Monica let loose with an oath more suitable to one of his palace stablehands. Never in a million years had he expected to hear that kind of language from such a petite woman. Although, he acknowledged silently, why he assumed size mattered, he couldn't understand.

"Isn't it a bit early to be thinking of Valentine's?"

Melanie shook her head. "Not at all. It's one of the biggest events on the local social calendar and raises thousands of pounds for the riding school. Will you stay long enough to attend?" With a wave of her hand, Melanie began again. "Strike that. I don't want to pressure you into any kind of commitment while you're on holiday."

"Even if I decide to do some travelling, I'll make sure I am back in time for your dance," Henri promised. "Tell me about it."

Melanie looked about her, spotted a lone bale of hay on the ground, and dropped down on it. "As I said, it's the biggest annual event in the area. We contact all the commercial businesses near and far, hit on all the local and not-so-local farmers for sponsorship. We have a core of a dozen families or so who are prepared to sit on the committee and as the day approaches, they all but desert their families in order to bring everything in on time.

"The dance is in the evening, but the events for the children begin mid-morning and continue right through the day. We hold riding competitions, party games, and in the afternoon we have a sports event."

"Sports?" Amazement and disbelief warred for

supremacy.

"Of course they are adapted to the children's needs, but just because they do not enjoy the same physical abilities of other children, it doesn't mean they lose their competitive spirit. Indeed not." She laughed. "You wait and see. I won't say it gets bloodthirsty out there, but it's not far off."

"No wonder you start so early," Henri murmured.

"This isn't the start, more the start of the final leg." Melanie chortled. "We start again the day after the dance."

"How many locals run the other way when they see you coming?" Already a firm admirer of his sister-in-law's abilities, Henri's respect and appreciation rose another notch. "And did you get involved while you worked for my father?"

"Of course!" Indignation laced her voice. "Obviously not as much as I would have liked," she said, then added, tongue in cheek, "your father is always very generous to our cause." Her lips twitched. "I hope I haven't frightened you away."

"Not at all," Henri denied, and wondered whether she heard the lie.

When he visited town with Liam, he'd been amazed at the friendly camaraderie between his brother and the locals. For security reasons, the truth of Liam's identity was known only to a select few officials. It didn't take the locals long to include Henri in their circle. The lack of the English pomposity astounded him, and when he made a comment he was soundly put in his place. "We are not English," had been the pithy reply. "We are Scots."

Monica's pale and serious face ended the conversation when she rejoined them in the barn.

Rising, Melanie held out her hands to her partner. "What is it? What's wrong?"

"Janice Carter," Monica replied.

Henri watched the colour drain from Melanie's face until it matched Monica's pallor.

"James is taking her to Switzerland tonight. She's asked that we go over before she leaves." Both women checked their watches.

"Did you call Rosie? Can she come over?"

"I did, and she will."

Neither woman included him in the conversation. Not, he was sure, from rudeness, but simply because they focussed totally on the subject at hand.

"Is there anything I can do?" he offered.

When they both looked up with wide, surprised eyes, he knew he'd guessed correctly. "I take it a friend of yours is in trouble."

"Yes." They both spoke at once before Monica continued. "James and his wife Janice are silent partners in the school."

At his raised eyebrow, Melanie elaborated. "We didn't have enough money when we started out and the banks refused to back us. James and Janice's first child had spina bifida and they heard us venting in the local coffee house after we left the bank. They supplied the necessary funds and became physically involved until Janice was diagnosed with a virulent form of cancer three months ago."

"Hardly the time to travel to Switzerland, surely?" Why would a man take his wife on a plane journey when she was clearly so ill? Then he remembered. The name eluded him, but he recalled the hazy details about the world-renowned clinic that aided the terminally ill.

"It is what she wants and what James promised to do for her." Monica's voice broke and without thinking he reached for her, pulling her against his chest. He'd given little thought to circumstances such as James and Janice's before, and now found his sympathies equally split between husband and wife.

Unsure what to say, he didn't try, just held her and let her scent drift into his awareness. His hand caressed the back of her head and down her back and up again in a soothing motion. Her shoulders shook for a second before she stiffened in his arms.

"I mustn't cry," she said, and stepped back. "Thank you. I don't want to arrive there with red eyes."

"You must know from Liam that I can ride and taught him and our other two brothers. If there is anything I can do..." He let the offer hang in the air.

"Would you?" Melanie offered him a sad smile. "Rosie is a wonderful teacher but we have two children booked in today, Charlie-Boy and Cressie. No way can she cope with both of them."

"Of course." Henri caught Monica's hand to prevent her from leaving. "I know you want to be gone, but tell me about the child I'm to help."

"Cressie? She is seven and the victim of a drunk-driving accident. There is hope she may regain mobility in her legs, and the horse riding is part of her therapy. She will plead for you to let her try the jumps, but simply tell her we asked that she not attempt them while we are away. That way you are off the hook when she moans."

Henri wondered if the charity's liability insurance would cover his help if an accident occurred while he was overseeing the children. "Will she?"

"Will she what? Oh! Moan? Most definitely. She has more spunk than is good for her and would run before she can walk if we let her. She's finding it hard to pace out her recuperation."

"A fighter?"

"Most definitely," Melanie repeated, with a full-blown smile this time. "And a charmer. Watch your step!"

Monica placed her hand over his. "Thank you," she said, and was gone.

January 18

The rhythmic sound of the dishwasher humming in the background lulled Monica into a sense of pleasant seclusion.

She understood Liam's joy when he discovered his brother had agreed to visit over Christmas, and his delight when Henri extended his stay. She'd assumed the wretched man meant another day or two, not a whole month, with no sign of an imminent departure.

She grabbed a kitchen paper towel and fanned her suddenly over-warm cheeks. The heir to the throne was picture-book perfect. Slightly taller than Liam, broader shoulders and leaner hips; how did the guy get so lucky? And how did she, silly chit that she was, lose her heart to Henri the Unobtainable?

The evening before the renewal of his brother's wedding vows, he'd never turned up for the rehearsal. "Pressure of work," the king had told them with a scowl. And the next day, during the ceremony, what did she go and do? Only give away her heart to a man standing what seemed like half a mile away at the other end of their massive cathedral aisle, that's all. One second, that was all it had taken. One lousy little second and she'd lost control of her own life.

The instant connection flowing between them had zapped her heart and took it hostage. Flummoxed by her reaction, she'd nearly fallen flat on her face. The potential humiliation stiffened her spine, and by the time she reached the steps of the altar, she'd convinced herself she'd imagined it all. After all, the whole place would intimidate better people than herself, she vowed.

Henri's jet-black hair gleamed like polished obsidian beneath the sunshine streaming through the cathedral windows. The ends kissed the collar of his tux. She'd read about chiselled features, high cheekbones, and eyes that gleamed with the promise of—. Now she knew the writers of her romance novels had it right.

She swallowed at the memory. If ever a man looked right in a tux! Prince Henri could have been born in the thing, it suited him so well. No collar-pulling for the prince. Liam, on the other hand, looked as though his collar would choke him before his bride arrived if he didn't look out. Purposefully ignoring the heir to the throne, Monica remembered smiling at Liam, making a slicing motion across her throat with one finger and sharing a laugh with him seconds before Liam spotted his bride and almost swallowed his tongue.

After that the memories merged until the moment the bridesmaid and best man stood up for their dance together.

And that obligatory dance?

It surprised her that he hadn't scorched holes through her dress where he held her. Her back tingled at the memory while her fingers shredded the paper kitchen towel she'd plucked from the roll. She threw the scraps of shredded tissue into the bin and grabbed another off the roll.

She'd never wanted it to end and wished it had never started. The feel of his arms around her, the woodsy scent of his cologne, even the haughty reserve in his eyes when he looked down at her, still sparked her blood and haunted her dreams.

And then she'd walked in to find him perched on the arm of Melanie's chair before Christmas...

His scathing rejection hurt, invoked too many memories she'd thought long buried.

Since her father's rejection, she'd vowed never to trust another man other than her brother, Billy. She'd loved him as a boy, loved him still as a man, and never envisaged trusting her heart to anyone else. Certainly not to a man beyond her station in life, one who made it clear he agreed with her estimation. Could she be any more stupid? She doubted it.

"You say that now," Melanie had declared to her when Liam and Henri left the women together to finalise their Christmas preparations. "You wait. Love happens. One minute you are heart-whole and the next..." Her eyes misted over. "Well, you know we had our moments, some of them so bad we nearly didn't make it." Melanie had paused in her effort to wrap her final present before placing it under the tree. "It hits you in the eye, or the heart, before you realise and then it's too late to do anything about it."

The second kitchen towel went the way of the first as she banished Melanie's prediction.

The sound of the dishwasher impinged on her memories. "Well, I'm not for turning," she said aloud, in an effort to deny her reaction at the sight of Henri sitting on the arm of Melanie's chair, his arm resting along the back of it, his face lit up at something Melanie had said. He'd looked up and her stomach flip-flopped, her heart had lurched into her throat, and her eyes wanted to feast on the sight of the man forever, until he cast her a scathing look and accused her of ruining his life!

Too stunned to defend herself, she'd stood rooted to the spot, her mouth agape, she was sure. *Ruined his life?* The jerk accused her of ruining his life! More like saving it, if all she'd heard was true.

Fortunately, so far, Henri had attached himself to his brother and appeared to spend his whole time dissecting business minutiae of the riding school and farm, and she'd seen nothing of him.

Well, almost.

Yesterday, unaware he was already there, she'd walked into the stables with the intention of riding round the lake. He'd been saddling up the mount Liam had offered him and looked up when she entered. Caught in the depth of his gaze, she'd failed to retreat quickly enough.

"I'm—" He waved one hand at his mount. "—taking the lakeside route if anyone asks for me."

In response she swallowed a curse... or thought she had.

"You have a problem with that?"

The dangerous glitter in his eyes had mesmerised her. She'd never met anyone like him before, and hated the effect he had on her heart. If, in a moment of madness, he suggested an affair, she just might agree, simply because he brought the devil out in her. Monica sighed at the absurdity of the idea. She wasn't that kind of girl, but the kind of girl she was might mean the only chance of having a child might be adoption, because no man she'd met so far hung about when they found out about her gift.

"No. No problem," she had said through gritted teeth. Soon it would be too dangerous to take the hill path, but she'd go that way instead of round the lake as planned. Without another word she headed for Raven, her preferred mount, and began saddling him up.

She hadn't realised Henri had followed her until he spoke, and his voice right at her back startled her into almost dropping the tackle.

"You're going riding?"

"Well, I'm not going dancing," she said, glancing at the tack in her hands.

"Where?"

"Don't worry, I have no intention of intruding upon your space; you are quite safe from me."

"That's not an answer. If you're not going round the lake, where are you going?"

How did he manage that 'royal' tone without moving a single facial muscle?

"I'm taking the hill route." Turning to her horse, she continued to work.

"I'm sure Liam mentioned it is not a path to use at this time of year."

"I don't need Liam's recent knowledge of the local terrain to inform me of the dangers. I'll tell you what I told your brother when he first arrived; the hill path during and immediately after snowy weather is out of bounds." She noted the fury in his eyes. Probably few people spoke to him with a directness matching his own, and the guy was having a hard time finding himself on the receiving end. "Liam is right inasmuch that if we get the predicted snow in the next couple of days, we will close the path off altogether."

He cocked his head to one side in a manner she'd come to recognise as when he was weighing up a person, situation, or comment.

"You'd better come with me."

Before she knew it, he set her aside and finished saddling her horse with an arrogance that set her blood boiling.

So how had she ended up riding side by side with him round the lake? Electrical sparks shot up her leg straight into her heart when their legs bumped together, and she almost fell out of the saddle.

At first, it irritated her when he took the lead as the path narrowed, without asking whether she wanted to go first, but a few minutes later she blessed his arrogance. She had the best view in the world. He'd refused the riding hat she offered him and now she watched his hair flying in the wind whipping across the water. His rhythmic movement meshed with his horse, poetry in motion. *Oh, the power in man and beast as they synchronise their movements.* The image of him on top of her flashed through her mind and was not helped by the steady pounding of hoofbeats beneath her. She groaned at her body's reaction to the images flashing through her mind, combined with the horse's rhythm.

Her throat had turned dry, her heart hammered in her chest, and her mind wandered to thoughts of his hands roaming over her body. *Lust,* she thought. Nothing more than lust, and wishful thinking, she told herself, and made a shocking discovery. That the last time she'd contemplated the possibility, she'd come to no firm conclusion.

This time...?

If the man offered a holiday romance, she *would* accept.

Stunned by her discovery, she'd jabbed at the reins and her horse nearly ran into the back of his.

"Are you all right?" Genuine concern shone from his eyes instead of the expected disparagement. His fingers, when he swung his horse 'round to grip her arm, were gentle, not biting.

"I'm sorry." Mortified, she leaned back in an attempt to free her arm. "I became distracted."

His eyes narrowed, his lips curved up, and she noticed the laugh lines 'round his eyes deepen.

"Well, it can't be the view," he said, and all she heard was the laughter in his voice.

"The view's incredible." She slapped her hand

over her mouth and prayed for the ground to open up and swallow her whole.

Henri's grin turned feral, then earnest. "Is it?" He leaned forward until his gaze, dark and intense, was inches away from hers. "I didn't dare ride behind you for fear of giving in to temptation and hauling you off your horse to the ground and ravishing you."

"Ravishing?" Was that hope she heard in her voice, or invitation, or fantasy? "That's a very old-fashioned word."

"At heart I'm an old-fashioned kind of guy."

She doubted that.

He leaned in and covered her mouth with his. Firm, seeking, demanding. She didn't know who was doing what, just let herself fall into the kiss, into the moment. The scent of his aftershave mingled with the taste of his lips. His tongue sought and conquered, then demanded a tango.

The wind moaned around them. No, not the wind... Monica's low growl of need. The reins dropped from her hands, allowing her to tunnel her fingers through his hair. She fisted her hands in its thickness and pulled him closer.

When he cupped one hand round the back of her head, she leaned into his other hand as it moved up from her waist. With a sigh, Monica let her hands drop and roam over his back.

"The moment I saw you—" he mapped her face with his lips before stopping long enough to add, "— I wanted you."

His hands dropped away, leaving a chill in their place.

"You don't sound very happy about it." She drew away and gasped for breath.

"I'm not. I wasn't," he corrected. "When I discovered you'd been behind the disruption of my life, I thought I'd never forgive you." His hand left her hair and cupped one cheek, his thumb caressing her lips.

Her body trembled with need. Fire, deeply seated, threatened to consume her. "And now?" If he asked, would she truly say yes to an affair?

"And now I know you've turned my life upside down and I'm not sure what to do about it." He paused, cocked his head to one side again, swore when his horse sidled away from hers, then gathered up the reins. "This is neither the time nor the place for this discussion." Irritation sparked in his eyes. "When we get back," he said and urged his horse forward.

Why this sudden change from ardent lover to cold and distant promises that sounded more like threats? Not sure, Monica remained where she was and watched the distance between them grow before wheeling her own mount around. She retraced the path back to the farm, her mind and body in turmoil.

Three

"Rosie is schooling Charlie-Boy this morning." Melanie picked up her car keys with one hand, scooped Jonathon out of Liam's arms with the other, and swooped out the kitchen door with a shout over her shoulder. "I'll be back this afternoon, Monica."

"And I'll see you in a couple of days," Liam said to the empty space, a whimsical grin on his face.

"Oh!" Melanie rushed back inside. "I forgot. Have fun at the horse auctions." She planted a smacking kiss on her husband's lips and vanished outside before anyone else could say a word.

"Thanks, hon." Liam swigged the last of his coffee, grinned at his brother, and rose. "You ready?"

Henri nodded and the two brothers left the kitchen together. Monica watched them cross the yard in the direction of the garage, then settled in to clear the breakfast dishes and start the laundry. She didn't mind one bit.

Billy had frequently scolded her for cleaning up after Melanie and Liam.

With a wave to Rosie as their most qualified volunteer led Charlie-Boy and his pony out into the exercise paddock, she placed the last plate in the dishwasher and snicked the door shut.

"If you're not careful, they'll start taking you for

granted," Billy had warned last time he visited. She'd laughed it off and assured him she didn't mind. Only today she did. The sight of the Gasquet family going about their business, serene in their companionship, brought a cold lump to her throat.

The laundry basket was full to overflowing with Henri's additional contribution. She fingered the black silk shirt; it was the same shirt he'd worn the night she first saw him at the farm. The soft silk against her cheek heated her blood as she inhaled his woodsy aroma. One of his favourites, she assumed, unless he had more than one, because he wore it often along with his designer jeans and black ankle boots.

A year ago, Melanie's job kept her away from the farm and school for more time than she was at it, and now... Monica sighed. Perhaps Billy had a point, and she'd have to sit down with Melanie sometime soon and discuss the changes and what it meant to their partnership.

Not before the Valentine Fair and dance, Monica thought. *Soon... immediately after...*

"Miss Mon'ca!"

The sound of the child's cry lent wings to Monica's feet. She shot through the kitchen door, down the steps, and round the corner to the nearest paddock. She expected to see Rosie leading the child's pony 'round the arena. Instead, the sight of the child clinging to the pony's neck, his face hidden in the animal's wind-blown mane, sent chills of fear down her spine.

Charlie-Boy, her neighbour's three-year-old son, screamed again. "I wan' Mon'ca!"

"What's the matter, baby?" Keeping the fear from her voice, she reached up and let the child tumble down from the saddle into her arms.

"Tubby's sick."

"He is?"

Charlie-Boy nodded, his red-rimmed eyes large and fearful. "He nearly falled and I thought I was going to get squashed."

"And what did Rosie do?"

"She's not here any more." Charlie-Boy sniffed and wiped his nose with the back of his chubby little hand.

"Did she say where she was going?" Monica assumed the child had misunderstood and her volunteer had gone to the stables for something.

"Her bell wang and she cried and ran to her car. I got fwightened. And Tubby tripped and I thought he was going to fall."

The bell, Monica knew, was Charlie-Boy's name for a phone.

What had happened to cause one of her most reliable volunteers to forget the basic rule of handing over to another adult before leaving a disabled child unattended, whether mounted on a horse or not? She cast a bemused glance in the direction of the empty drive.

"Now he's sick." Charlie-Boy's hand cupped her chin, snatching her attention again.

"What?" She looked across at the pony, standing head-down and leaning against the fence near the gate, with one foot raised off the ground.

With a sigh, she wished Melanie hadn't gone into town. She couldn't leave Charlie-Boy, and while she remained on her own she couldn't tend to the pony either.

"I need to get my bell, Charlie-Boy." Resting him on her hip, she strode back to the house. Half of her hoped Melanie would return early; the other half knew she didn't intend to return before mid-afternoon. Liam would be gone for two days.

She didn't have time to go looking for him, and

snatched up her mobile phone to speed-dial Court, the vet.

He'd taken a month off immediately after Christmas, but she hoped he'd be back early. But luck, it seemed, was not smiling on her today. Even his locum did not pick up. She left a message on the answering machine, and with Charlie-Boy's arms locked round her neck in a stranglehold, retraced her steps.

"I've got to put you in your chair, Charlie-Boy," she said, keeping a smile on her lips and in her voice. "Poor Tubby needs a little help from me and I can't hold you while I work on him."

Before Charlie-Boy could fully scrunch up his little face in readiness for a loud protest, Monica kissed his nose. "Watch very carefully because one day when you are all grown up, you might want to help animals when they are poorly." Not waiting for a response, Monica strapped him in his chair and set it where she could keep her eye on it and its occupant.

"Well, now then, Tubby, your day is no better than mine, is it? Let's see what I can do for you until we can get hold of the vet."

Offering a sugar lump to the distressed animal, she ran a hand over his shoulders and up his neck and back again in rhythmic strokes. When Tubby relaxed, she moved in and ran her hands over the injured leg. She ignored the pony's warm breath on her neck, talking softly, all the while moving her hand over the area of the injury, scanning for disturbances in the animal's energies.

She observed Charlie-Boy watching her and smiled. Somehow his open curiosity helped her reach that inner calmness, the almost meditative state needed to connect on an energetic level with the pony.

"It always surprises me," she told the child, "that while people happily accept that radio and TV both need an arial to receive the frequencies that provide the signal and pictures, they shy away when someone tries to explain that healing works in the same way."

Charlie-Boy nodded as though he understood everything she was doing. Perhaps he did. Even scientists admitted children were more open to such things than adults.

"Unlike people, animals never lost that sixth sense and can tune into it far more readily, far more naturally. Isn't that so, Tubby?"

The pony whickered at the sound of his name, turned his head, and tried to nudge her shoulder.

"You know healing can only do good and can never cause harm, don't you, boy?" She shifted position, moved her hands, waited until Tubby settled again, and focussed on helping to relieve the animal's pain.

She never claimed to heal any injury, just to relieve the pain and give comfort to the animal. Conventional treatments she left to the owners and the vets alike, many of whom claimed she'd reversed negative situations in the past. Once she had cringed at the praise offered; now she'd learned to accept it with humility and made no attempt to benefit from their claims.

She couldn't explain how she understood what animals told her, couldn't explain why she saw things when she sat in front of her fire at night. Nor could she verbalise the soul-deep satisfaction of being a small part in a creature's recovery.

After a while, the vibration beneath her hands increased, morphing into a cold draft emanating from the animal's leg, and then warmed again. The energies levelled out, becoming calmer. Tubby nickered and moved.

"Whoa, boy." The deep, rich tone of Henri's voice right behind her sent a different kind of vibration thundering through Monica's body. If hearts could jump, she swore hers would have leaped right out of her chest. Not just from fright at being taken unawares, but because of the magnetism sparking between them when they were close. *Not even close,* she thought, and wondered again how he'd managed to approach without her internal antennae picking him up. And, she wondered, how much had he heard of her explanation to Charlie-Boy?

"Whatever you are doing seems to be helping the pony." Henri hunkered down beside her and watched the steady, deliberate movement of her hands.

"Mon'ca." Charlie's now fractious tone sliced through the last of her fading concentration.

She gave Tubby a final pat and stepped back from him. Henri's presence, and Charlie's mounting irritation at being ignored, triggered the protective shield she wrapped around herself when strangers discovered her gift.

Even though they knew about it, Monica didn't enjoy her friends or Court, the vet, watching her work. Old habits died hard, she told herself, but knew she feared a resurgence of the childhood rejection she'd experienced.

"He seems easier." Like soft velvet, Henri's voice cloaked her in reassuring warmth.

"Yes. I think it will turn out to be a strain, but I've called Court."

"Court?"

"The vet."

"Where's your volunteer?" Henri's glance focussed on the barn, and Monica shook her head.

"I don't know. Charlie-Boy said she got a phone call and rushed off."

"Is that normal for her?"

"No." Shaking her head, Monica's anger towards Rosie wavered. Whatever prompted the uncharacteristic action from her most trusted volunteer, she could, this time, wait for an explanation before ripping the woman's reputation to shreds. "She should've called me before abandoning Charlie. It's a miracle the child didn't fall off." A shudder ripped through her while her mind created a video of the nonexistent disaster of Charlie flying through the air and crashing to the ground. His screams seemed so real she covered her ears.

Henri's firm grip on her arms as he gently shook her snapped her out of her daylight nightmare.

"It didn't happen."

Did he know what was going on inside her head? Unable to formulate the words, she settled for a shake of her head.

"Mon'ca!" Charlie's cries for attention increased in volume. "I'm thirsty."

She fought for a smile when she wanted to cry. *Reaction,* she acknowledged, and unbuckling his safety strap, swooped him into the air before settling him back on her hip.

"I'll have to tell his father," she said, and pushed the kitchen door open. The aroma of freshly brewed coffee greeted her. "Will you take Charlie? You'll find his beaker of milk on the counter beside the kettle." She passed the child to Henri before he opened his mouth to protest, and left the two males staring at each other with equal measures of misgiving.

January 25

For the last week it seemed to Monica that Henri went out of his way to avoid her. She wished she could dismiss him with a similar ease.

She should have been working on the mammoth lists of tasks still to be done for the annual all-day Valentine celebration. Instead she'd treated herself to a walk down to the lakeside, and now sat with her arms wrapped 'round her up-drawn legs and her chin resting on her knees, watching the sunlight dance on the crest of the wind-swept waves. She relished the unusual warmth of the sun for the time of year, and angled her body to let the heat ease the taut muscles in her back.

She'd spent the morning mucking out the horse stalls while the volunteers worked with the children. Her body craved the physical exercise to work off her rising frustration. Frustration at herself and what she perceived as her weakness towards the prince, and intensified by her longing for the feel of his hands on her body. His lips on hers. The warmth of his breath skimming across the surface of her face, her throat — and she conceded with a groan, that wouldn't be nearly enough.

She wanted his hands, and more, much more than the touch of his hands roaming all over her. How come, when she dreamed of him, his lips caressing every inch of her, it seemed as real as the sensation of her fingers running through the coarse lakeside grass beside her?

She ignored the approaching hoofbeats when she first heard them. Plenty of horse riders used the lakeside route as a regular form of exercise. Awash with rampant desire for a man she could never have, she didn't notice the silence when the rider reined in his horse and dismounted beside her.

"May I join you?" Henri's usually smooth voice turned husky. His eyes darkened with desire while he waited for her consent. Joy filled her heart. The sparks that flew between them were acknowledged and reciprocated in those fleeting seconds before reality kicked in.

Her desires might be as real and hot as a raging inferno, but she and the prince were as different as chalk and cheese.

He'd dropped down beside her before she gathered enough wits to stop him.

"Why have you been avoiding me?"

Direct! Always direct, Monica thought, while searching for a pithy response and finding none. He'd not been the only one playing the avoidance game.

"I could ask you the same thing," she said instead. "I simply took my cue from you."

"No, you didn't." His contradiction came swift and sharp. "If you had, you would be in my arms by now."

Ignoring her jubilant heart, she strove for prim. "I beg your pardon?"

"Don't play games with me." In amazement, she watched as the suave prince morphed into a frustrated man. "From the second you walked down the aisle, I've wanted you."

"You soon recovered, it seems. Your first words to me when you got here were a string of threats."

He shifted in uneasy acknowledgement of her hit. "I did recover," he said, and took hold of her clasped hands. "I did recover," he repeated. "And for that I am sorry. My world had just turned upside down and I needed someone to blame."

"And lucky little me was it." She tugged to free her hands and succeeded only in allowing him to tighten his grasp.

Temper sparked in his eyes. "I've said I'm sorry. Do you want me to prove it?"

She didn't see him move.

One moment he glowered at her, the next his

kiss threatened to incinerate her. Taken unaware, she gasped her protest, and he sucked it in as his tongue dove into her mouth.

He tasted of the honey and toast he'd eaten at breakfast, of the strong coffee he preferred, while the woodsy scent of his cologne captured her senses. Her lips sought more. Before the signal left her brain, her hands went on an exploration of their own. Rolling her onto her knees, he carried her with him when he fell onto his back. She sighed with pleasure when her body flattened against the hardness of his chest and her common sense decided to take an instant sabbatical.

His hair was softer than she remembered; his face sharper, more angular than when he'd arrived. She let her lips follow in the wake of her hands as they mapped the angles of his face, skimmed over his nose and down to his throat.

When they reached his racing pulse, her heart sighed and slammed a lock on her brain before her common sense returned. Somewhere in the deepest, darkest corner of her mind, she knew heartbreak would follow this insanity, but ignored it. Never before had a man's touch inflamed her passion as Henri's did. She revelled in the knowledge that for once in her life she'd let go of her inhibitions and let her feelings off the leash.

In the distance, lightning split dense grey clouds.

She stiffened for a second when he tugged at her T-shirt until he expertly distracted her with his lips. The feel of his lean fingers against her back fanned the flames of her desire and she wriggled on top of him.

"Do you know what you are doing to me, woman?"

Never having tagged herself as passionate, she

rejoiced in it now. His voice, rough with desire, simply drove her wild for more. *Much* more.

"I want you."

An overhead clap of thunder drowned out her jubilant admission and retrieved her scattered wits. Shocked at her wanton behaviour, she scrambled back and found herself straddling him, her hands once more locked in his. His heaving chest matched hers as they stared at each other.

His eyes, so full of desire and passion, turned cold. The seconds stretched out between them, pinning them in place until another clap of thunder roared across the sky directly above them.

Without ceremony, Henri rolled over, sending her flying onto her back. He scrambled to his feet, and instead of reaching out to help her up, he leaned down, his hands fisted on his hips.

"Do you appreciate how close you came to me taking you here and now?" He indicated the wide open spaces with an arc of his arm.

She swore his voice out-growled the muttering thunder. Lightning slashed between them and she scrambled to her feet. Thunder she could tolerate, but lightning? No, she didn't like lightning at all.

Still gasping for breath, she stepped back, and realised her mistake too late when the cold slap of water against her heel slopped into her sturdy working shoe. Instead she strove to emulate his stance by planting her fists on her hips. "May I remind you I didn't start this?" Blinking away the threatening tears, she held herself rigid in the face of his fury. What right did he have to take the moral high road? She wasn't the one who'd thrown herself at him.

"This? *This!*" He leaned into her face and Monica resisted the urge to retreat again. "What we had going a second ago was more than just *this*," he snapped.

"Really?" Shaking from equal measures of reaction to Henri's lovemaking a moment ago, his dismissal now, and the storm, Monica decided to go for broke. "Other than lust, what would you call it?"

"Opportunistic," he said, then turned the air blue with a string of foreign curses.

She'd expected a quick retort, not the blank look that was quickly followed by bewilderment. She expected him to grip her arms and shore up his comments, not to retreat in the manner she'd just resisted. Nor had she expected the knife-sharp stab to her heart his words inflicted.

Opportunistic? He thought she was deliberately trying to entice him so he'd offer her — what? She'd been minding her own blasted business when he turned up and all but threw himself on her; well, no, she was on top of him, but he'd pulled her there when he toppled backwards.

Paralyzed with shock, she stood and gaped at his retreating back as fat drops of rain splattered at her feet. She watched Henri cast a glance 'round for his horse and stride away from her without another word. He didn't look back when he mounted and set off towards the farm. And she ignored the deluge of rain that soaked her clothes and plastered her hair to her face.

She welcomed the cool water and remained where she stood while it quenched the raging inferno within. Turning her face upward, she noticed the angry yellow clouds edged with charcoal grey scudding across the sky. Another prolonged roll of thunder and simultaneous flashes of lightning energised her and she ran for cover. Not into the barn, but up to the spare room above it that doubled as a flat-cum-bolthole when she needed privacy and thinking time, or for some reason couldn't make the return journey home.

Wherever she went, she knew she wouldn't be alone. Embarrassment, humiliation, and guilt over her uncharacteristic behaviour would stalk her, like shadows, for a long time to come.

That should never have happened. She didn't need to hear the words to know he'd uttered them on his way to his horse.

"As usual, Your Highness, you are quite right," she said, now to the roiling clouds. "It should never have happened, but—" She took a deep breath. "—it took two, so don't go trying to shift all the blame."

January 30

"Did Rosie ever explain the reason for her unauthorised departure the other day?" Melanie wiped her son's face and hands. "I'm just thankful Charlie-Boy's father didn't skin us alive."

"I thought you knew." Monica took the cloth from Melanie and rinsed it under the tap. Sunlight streamed through Melanie's kitchen window. "Rosie's father had a massive heart attack. She made it home with minutes to spare." She loaded the dishwasher with breakfast dishes.

"Oh!" Jogging her son on her hip, Melanie paced the room and back again. "How come I didn't know anything about this? According to Liam, Henri offered to take over in Rosie's absence. I thought he was joining Liam at the auction."

"So did I," Monica said, and pretended not to see the speculative glance Melanie shot in her direction. "Are you busy this afternoon?" Monica asked as she rinsed the cloth again.

"Not especially. Why?"

"Because if we don't get together to tie up the last few items on our list, we'll still be dealing with them during the Valentine Bonanza."

Melanie stared at the now sleeping child in her arms, a soft smile curving her lips. Motherhood suited her friend, Monica thought, refusing to acknowledge the spurt of envy licking at her heart. Squeezing the cloth, she draped it over the tap and headed for the back door. "I have stable work to do. I'll see you in the sitting room after lunch. In the meantime—" She paused, her hand on the doorknob. "If you have time to contact Round Haven House and find out what their final contributions towards the food will be, it will be a big help."

The committee members had blasted her ear off the previous day, wanting the information, and Monica knew Henri was on the office phone to his palace officials. Hopefully he wouldn't take all morning. In the meantime, the committee members would just have to wait: she didn't want another confrontation with the prince.

The sting of hot water showering over her body eased her aching muscles. Monica wished it would do the same for her heart. Why, oh why, couldn't she dismiss Henri from her mind? She'd long given up on her heart. It seemed to have a will of its own, and nothing she tried persuaded it that Henri was bad news.

For every detail awaiting her personal attention, two more seemed to take their place the nearer the Valentine's Day event came. Normally she relished the challenge, but this year, knowing Henri would fly home the following day, robbed her of all her enthusiasm. *Take tonight,* she reminded herself with disgust; she'd left a raft of folders on her desk and, thinking she'd placed them in her briefcase, had come home without them. If she wanted to get the work done, it meant returning to pick them up and working through most of the night.

Her doorbell peeled as she stepped from the shower and reached for a towel. Praying it was Melanie with her files, she wrapped the towel around her, slipped on her robe, and ran for the hallway, ignoring the water running off her hair and soaking the back of her robe. Out of breath, she swung the door open.

"You left these behind. Melanie said you'd need them tonight," Henri said, shoving the missing files at her.

If she took them, she'd lose the towel, and if she didn't, she'd have to ask him in.

Modesty won out; it wasn't a hard decision, she told herself as she stepped back to let him in.

"She's right, I do. Thank you." She stepped back and indicated the partially open door to her left. "Come in. I'll be back in a moment." She headed for her bedroom at the back of the flat, then stopped in the doorway when he spoke.

"I'm not staying."

"No, I understand." *Better than you think.* The errant thought twanged at her conscience. He had, after all, come out to bring the files to her, thus saving her at least an hour's journey there and back, plus general chit-chat time. This way, Henri could pass on any messages Melanie had for her and then leave.

Five minutes later, in jeans and a chunky sweater of vibrant purple, Monica rejoined her visitor.

"Thank you for bringing these." She indicated the folders Henri had placed on the coffee table.

"Not a problem."

He wasn't seated on one of her chairs as she expected, nor was he studying her books or music collection. If he'd spent time looking at her photographs of Billy, he never mentioned them. No, he was squatting on the floor in front of her cheery fire.

"Don't you find having a real fire too much work? After all, you're out all day, so it must take a while before you benefit from the heat."

"I enjoy a real fire." No need to tell him about the things she read in the flames. "It has its own energy. You don't get the same ambience from a gas or electric fire, and radiators discreetly placed may be eminently logical but do nothing for me."

When he made no move to leave, she fetched two glasses from her minuscule kitchen, poured white wine in both, and offered him one. "No point in offering you a choice because this is all I've got," she said with a deprecating smile.

"Just what I would have chosen," he said, and settled more cosily on the floor.

With a sigh of inevitability, Monica settled down beside him, rattled at his apparent ability to put the events of the previous week out of his mind — and wary about revealing too much of herself, given his poor opinion of her.

For the next hour Henri asked several questions about the riding school, their goals for the future, and she gradually relaxed and answered them happily.

"The only time some of these children are in control of their own lives, even to a limited extent, is when they are on a horse. Not only do they get to enjoy the power of personal achievement, they get a full-body muscle exercise, too."

Using their fingers to eat it, they'd shared a pizza, while sitting cross-legged on the floor. After disposing of the empty carton, she poured more wine and dropped down in front of the fire once more. Silence settled 'round them and she almost forgot his presence as she stared into the fire.

Without warning, a vision danced in the flames. A man, dandling a child on his knee; not just any man, but Henri. While her heart broke, she continued to study the images before her. He looked so happy. *A year.* The words sprang into her mind. *A year.* Did that mean he'd have a child within a year or that the child she saw was a year old?

She wanted a child, *his* child, she admitted; instead all she saw was Henri playing with a baby, and she knew it was his. She searched for the mother of the child and couldn't see her.

Frustration gnawed at her gut when the vision faded, and she looked around at the appalled expression on Henri's face.

"What?" she asked, but knew the answer. She had spoken aloud. Had voiced her vision.

"What kind of game are you playing?"

All trace of the tentative friendship they'd been building in the last hour evaporated.

"If this is some kind of attempt to blackmail me, you are whistling in the wind!"

"Blackmail?" Her brain seized, and she struggled to comprehend his accusations. "Why would I want to blackmail you?"

"You sit there staring into the fire and start babbling about me being married and having a child in twelve months." He shot to his feet and glowered down at her. "You must think I fell off a Christmas tree if you believe I'd fall for such an opportunistic load of balderdash. When I marry, it won't be to an avaricious witch like you."

He crossed the room so fast she didn't see him move — only knew he'd gone when she heard her front door slam.

She wondered how he could think such vile things about her and she hugged her arms around her shaking body. Once again her gift of reading the flames had caused her more heartache and rejection. And worst of all, she hadn't even realised she'd verbalised her visions. It didn't matter when she was on her own. Knowing she had no alternative, Monica pulled the Valentine's Day files towards her and began to work.

February 7

With one week left before the Valentine bonanza, Monica headed for the sitting room in search of Melanie. They needed to compare notes and see how many more things they could cross off their still-to-do list. She rushed through the door and came to a shuddering halt. Henri was slumped sideways in the chair, fast asleep, and there was no sign of Melanie.

With her fingers curling 'round the old-fashioned brass door knob, she studied the sleeping prince. Deep lines furrowed his brow. Did he still think of all those duties he'd been forced to lay to one side before coming to Scotland? Or did something else trouble the man?

Lashes women would kill for fanned his high cheekbones. He'd lost some of the fleshiness around his eyes that she associated with his lifestyle. With a huff, she hastily hid behind her hand and corrected herself. What did she know of his lifestyle? It couldn't be more different from her own, that much she *did* know. While he spent his life in the public eye most of the time, she discreetly channelled her gifts into helping the children who sought peace and confidence from the riding school program for disabled children. *No,* she corrected herself mentally, *physically challenged is the politically correct term these days.* They had a point, she acknowledged silently as the man in the chair shifted, sighed, and settled back into sleep.

In spite of the last words he'd thrown at her when he brought the folders to her flat, she still wanted to touch him. To skim her fingers through his hair, to brush her lips over his, to see the same longing in his eyes for her as the one that consumed her. She didn't know what drew her to Henri. The Unreachable, she'd nicknamed him, but he'd captured her heart almost the moment they'd first met.

Why couldn't she shut out these feelings? Only a fool or a wimp would lust after someone who'd considered her nothing more than an opportunistic tart.

The outdoor life he'd embraced since arriving at the farm accentuated his sharp bone structure, creating a lean, strong silhouette to his face. Not that it had ever been anywhere near weak, she admitted. Perhaps that was why her heart had cartwheeled 'round her chest when she had first set eyes on him. Her fingers tightened around the doorknob as her eyes travelled from his face to his broad shoulders, muscled chest, lean hips... and farther.

The sigh of settling logs in the fire refocussed Monica's attention, while she remained in the doorway for another second. She'd hoped he'd be out riding, as was his usual afternoon custom, and had expected to find her partner and friend in the office after she'd finished playing with Jonathon.

How had the man gotten beneath her defences? Hadn't she learned too often and too well that she always ended up getting hurt by letting people close? A compulsion stronger than her willpower drew her across the room until she stood beside his chair and inhaled the scent of his aftershave — not one of those heavy, overpowering ones the advertisers swore drew every woman for miles.

Why, when she found his brother Liam charming and witty, and knew she could always rely on his friendship, why did her heart have to go and fall at the feet of his brother, the heir of a small and immensely rich kingdom? Someone so far out of her social realm it was beyond laughable. The tear that trickled down her cheek drew a muttered oath from her lips, and to her horror Henri's eyes twitched and snapped open.

Too late, Monica realised she should have left the room instead of lingering at the doorway before crossing to stand beside his chair.

"What?" He angled a glance at her and clamped his hand on his neck while the air turned blue with his curses. Without waiting for her answer, he dug his fingers into the back and side of his neck and massaged the kinks to an accompaniment of grunts.

Allowing compassion to shunt her logic out the way, Monica moved to the back of his chair, pulled his hand away, and began, with gentle fingers, to massage his neck with the rhythmic movements she knew would ease his pain and release the trapped muscles.

The warmth beneath her fingers turned cold, revealing the extent of pain he experienced.

"You've been sleeping in the chair."

Great observation, girl, she told herself. As if he didn't know the awkward angle he'd ended up in was responsible for the crick in his neck. When he made to move away from her ministrations, she clamped one hand on his shoulder.

"Not yet. Give me another couple of minutes and it will ease."

She waited, unsure whether he'd relax or leave. When his body softened, she let out a sigh of relief. For another five minutes her fingers kneaded, dug, probed, and soothed in equal measures, and she allowed herself to revel in the touch. Nothing sexual, just their energies mixing, swirling between them, and settling. The rightness of the moment seeped into her soul, and before she could prevent them, images of a future together flipped across her mind, breaking the spell.

She allowed her hands to drift down his arms, and then she stepped back. A glance at the clock revealed the need for her to search for Melanie if she hoped to cross anything else off her to-do list today.

Before she'd taken a step, his fingers manacled her wrist. Emotion, too dark to interpret, filled his eyes.

"Thank you. I know from experience that it can take days, sometimes weeks for a crick like that to ease. It feels terrific." He rolled his head in a circle, stretching his neck, and offered her one of his heart-melting smiles.

As suddenly as a light turning off, his smile vanished. "But don't let it give you ideas, just because I let you ease my shoulder." His voice chilled the warmth from the room and sent shivers down her spine.

"As if," she muttered before almost running from the room. Why couldn't the stupid fool see that she'd take him in a heartbeat, even — *especially*, she corrected — if he had barely two pennies to rub together? It was the man's heart she wanted, not his wealth or his kingdom.

<h1 style="text-align:center">*Four*</h1>

February 7

Dreams were all very well for those who had time for them, but as heir to his father's throne, Henri had always considered dreams a waste of valuable time. Now? He wasn't sure of anything any more.

He stared into the empty space Monica had occupied only minutes before. Monica the dreamer, Monica the gentle, Monica... the woman he loved.

He loved her!

With the revelation, Henri expected his world to implode. After all, hadn't he just told her, if not with his usual directness, to take a hike? Hadn't he all but accused her of using her gift to ensnare his heart to gain social and financial security?

How could he have been so crass, so stupid, and so disrespectful?

He snorted in disgust. He'd been more than deliberately callous. He'd taken one look at her sparkling eyes, full of hope and love and — he cursed when the truth hit him — trust! Whether she'd known it at a conscious level, Monica had trusted him enough to give voice to her vision. He didn't have to like what she said. But to wantonly destroy and belittle her in such a way was cruel, and until this moment, Henri had always prided himself in his thoughtful and caring response to the women in his life. She'd trusted him when he visited her flat, and he'd deliberately set out to destroy that trust.

Why?

Because he'd been too afraid to admit that she was more than just another woman, too afraid to admit to loving her! All his life had been spent watching his parents, knowing theirs was an arranged marriage. To him, it epitomised everything he looked for in his own marriage. Why hadn't he seen it before? Theirs wasn't just a staid match made between countries. Beneath the façade they offered to the world, his parents' marriage was filled with warmth, closeness, and companionship, certainly. But now, from his time and experience with Monica, he recognised the love his parents shared. The true meeting-of-minds-and-hearts kind of love.

A log shifting in the fireplace behind him snapped him back to attention. The room closed around him; the ceiling caught the lengthening shadows and multiplied the ones growing in his heart. The warmth of the room stifled him. He needed fresh air and space, lots of space, and he couldn't find that inside the house.

Striding from the room, he was already running by the time he reached the kitchen door.

A horse. He needed a horse... What was that Shakespearean quote? *A horse, a horse! My kingdom for a horse!*

No way did he equate himself with the pathetic King Richard III. For one, he stood a little more than six-feet three-inches tall in his socks, with a ramrod straight back, unlike the hunchback of a ruler who reputedly hid his weaknesses behind a wall of arrogance.

He almost fell over his feet when he came to an

abrupt halt. Wasn't he guilty of weaknesses such as King Richard's? Hadn't he just lashed out at Monica in order to hide his growing emotions for her? Lust he'd had no problem with until this moment, and if he'd had his way, he'd have taken her at the lakeside weeks ago, without a thought for the future. Without any expectation of her standing at his side during his royal duties. Thank goodness the arrival of the thunderstorm had put a stop to it.

He'd been so entrenched in the expectation that his bride would come from the ranks of what people laughingly called the upper echelons of society; he'd never once, before now, considered the impact his behaviour would have on Monica.

Weakness and arrogance: he was guilty of both. He continued towards the stables, desperate for the open spaces and the freedom he'd find beyond the farm boundaries. He'd take the route 'round the lake and up into the hills, he decided. When a stable hand came forward to help him saddle up his mount, he waved the man away.

Anxious to outride his gremlins, Henri ignored the man's warnings of coming snow. Once he was well away from the barn, he urged his horse into a canter, and then an all-out gallop. Relishing the wind whipping through his hair, ignoring the gathering dark grey accumulations of clouds, Henri concentrated on the demons of guilt, shame, and self-disgust perched on his shoulder, unable to shake them off however fast he tried to elude them.

To the thunder of hoofbeats on frozen ground, Henri's thoughts swirled 'round in his brain. He wished he could turn back the clock, start the afternoon all over again. He wished he'd have the opportunity to tell Monica he loved her, but now — even if he did, she'd never believe him.

His breath misted in front of him, drifted up to

obscure his vision, and the next thing he knew he was flying through the air.

🐎

"What possessed Henri to take a horse out so late in the afternoon, let alone when a blizzard is forecast to hit the area?" Melanie paced the room, young Jonathon dozing in her arms. "And Monica? Where is she? The groom said Henri went out alone. And yet at lunch your brother told me he intended to ask Monica to ride out with him for an hour."

She came to an abrupt halt in front of her husband. "I told him we'd arranged to finalize the Valentine schedule and stuff, but he simply used that dismissive royal wave of his and told me it could wait!"

Henri's attempt to intimidate hadn't impressed her, and she simply sniffed, raised her chin, and held the baby out for Liam to take. "Here, look after Jon. I'm going over to see if Monica can shed some light on Henri's disappearance."

"They're adults, leave them alone," Liam advised as he bounced his son on his knee while holding another, important gurgling conversation with the baby.

"Yeah!" Melanie scoffed. "Like I would leave Henri out there with this blizzard coming in without at least finding out what happened and whether, if she refused his request to ride with him, your brother just may have taken the horse to go after Monica, though goodness knows why he couldn't use the four-by-four like a normal person in their own home. And you can bet money on it, your father will ring up and demand to speak to Henri just when we don't know where he is. What will you tell him then?"

The sound of the phone ringing split the silence,

and rocking back on her heels Melanie waved at it. "You can answer that. I'm outta here."

Grabbing her car keys, Melanie swept from the room, only stopping when she heard Liam shout her name.

"What?" She swung 'round in the doorway.

"Monica wants to talk to you. Says that starting on the fifteenth, she's taking the holiday she's owed for looking after the place when we 'left her in the lurch' — her words." He shrugged and handed the phone to her.

Something wasn't right. Monica did not just up and leave others high and dry like this. "Is Henri going with you?"

"You are joking, aren't you?"

The derision in Monica's voice had Melanie removing the phone from her ear and staring at it as if it had morphed into something demonic. "Why would I joke about something like that?" she asked, using indignation to push away her growing fear. "To the rest of us, it's obvious the two of you are nuts about each other."

"For a short while that's what I hoped — that Henri is nuts about me — but no, you're all wrong."

Monica's snap furrowed Melanie's brow. "Well, if he's not with you, where is he?"

"I neither know nor care."

Melanie heard the tapping of a keyboard filter through the ether. "Where are you going?"

"Whichever destination I can get a flight out to before nightfall."

"Do not even think of leaving your house before I get there." Seriously worried now, about both Monica and Henri, Melanie cut the call, then stalked back to where Liam sat with the baby.

"Henri is not with Monica, and she's threatening to leave tonight." She bent down and dropped a kiss on the baby's downy hair. "You need to report Henri's missing to the police—" She brushed her lips over Liam's. "—while I try to prevent Monica from running away." She straightened and tweaked Jon's nose, then huffed and headed for the doorway once more.

🐎

Monica stood back when Melanie stormed into her home and stalked straight past her into the kitchen before whirling around.

"What's going on between you and Henri?" Melanie demanded before Monica had a chance to protest at her friend's invasion.

"Nothing's going on." The slap of her hand on the countertop echoed between the friends. "Nothing's going on," Monica repeated. "He made it as clear as crystal he is not looking for any kind of relationship, let alone one between the two of us." When a tear trickled down her cheek, she swiped it away with the back of her hand. "Not even a tussle-beneath-the-sheets kind of relationship."

The shock on Melanie's face offered a rueful kind of satisfaction, but it didn't last long. The comforting warmth of Melanie's arm around her released the tears she'd held onto all afternoon. She sniffled. "I thought — I don't know what I thought, but I was wrong."

"The man's head-over-heels in love with you," Melanie stated. "A blind man could tell how you feel about him. You're not the kind of person who'd consider a fling of any kind unless you had feelings for the guy."

"Maybe so, but according to the gallant prince, I'm only after his title and the financial security he'd give me."

"He never said that!" Melanie shoved away from

her friend and stared into her tear-drenched eyes and pale face.

"To be precise, he told me he never pegged me for one of the 'scheming witch brigade,' so I have decided to give him what he wants and go away until he leaves."

Melanie tore a paper towel off the kitchen roll and passed it to her friend before filling the kettle and brewing a pot of tea. "When did he say this?"

"The night he brought those files over—" After she'd let her guard down and interpreted the visions she'd seen within the flames. "—and again today." And the irony? Now she remembered what she'd said to him while in the trancelike state.

"And he called you a scheming witch?" Melanie's voice shocked her back to the present. "Somehow I don't see him saying that."

"He accused me of being an opportunist and implied I was only interested in him for his wealth and position."

"His loss."

Melanie's sudden indifference startled Monica into studying her friend's face more closely. Something other than Melanie's anger at her brother-in-law bothered her.

"So you didn't go riding together?" Melanie reached into the cupboard for two cups and set them on the counter top.

"Riding? No, we didn't go riding." Monica's sour tone threatened to curdle the milk her friend took from the fridge.

"So where was he when you left?"

Monica watched Melanie pour a liberal quantity of milk into her cup and grimace when the tea hardly turned the milk brown.

"I don't like strong tea," Melanie said, "but how can you drink this peelly-wally brew?"

Monica recognised that irritation, fostered by more than just her dislike for Monica's tea, laced Melanie's voice, and she waited for her to set both cups on the table before answering.

"He was in the sitting room when I left." Shifting her focus from her drink, Monica stared across the table. "Why?"

"He's missing."

"And I should care?"

"Don't fake your feelings with me. Whatever has gone on between the two of you, you still care."

Monica crumpled. Tears streamed down her face, her shoulders slumped, and she dropped her head into her hands. "How do you stop loving someone?" she wailed. "I thought he understood."

Monica looked into her friend's mind and saw Melanie's desire to comfort her friend clash with her growing fear for her brother-in-law's safety.

"Right now your feelings are incidental. We know Henri took a horse out towards the lake, but we're not sure when."

"The stablehand..."

"Had already left for the day by the time we realised Henri was missing. He told the boy to remain behind until Henri returned. When darkness fell and Henri still hadn't come back the boy came to tell us."

Monica looked at her watch, gasped, and shot to her feet. "It's been dark for ages; what are you waiting for?" She headed for the hall, snatched up her coat, and started dragging it on.

"I'm waiting to get the facts so we can pin down more accurately how long Henri has been out before the storm hits," Melanie informed her, and pulled the front door closed behind them before heading to the car.

Neither spoke during the drive back to the farm. Monica watched her friend concentrate on the atrocious road conditions and battled against her own fears.

He was out there somewhere with the blizzard due to hit anytime soon and no one knew where. She might never see him again.

"Monica."

Henri's voice filled her head, filled the car, tremulous, carrying undercurrents of desperation with panic running through it.

Automatically she turned to the back of the car to speak to him. He wasn't there. A picture of him flashed in her mind and disappeared too quickly for her to take in the details. Only his emotions stayed with her. Fear, sorrow, determination in equal measures; even as she concentrated on them they began to fade out.

"Hurry!" She swung round and grabbed Melanie's arm, almost causing her to lose her grip on the steering wheel.

"Have a care, will you," Melanie shouted. "Next time you pull a stunt like that, we may end up in a ditch and find ourselves going nowhere at all."

"I heard him. He's alive. Oh, Melanie, I heard him. Hurry, he's out there and calling for me."

Snow began falling in earnest before they reached the farm and Monica's nerves shredded a bit more with each flake that landed on the already rock-hard ground.

"Why did the idiot go riding alone with a blizzard forecast for this evening?"

Melanie cast a derisive glance in her direction. "Probably for the same stupid reason you thought running off to some far distant corner of the world would solve all your problems." She dropped into a lower gear and eased the car round the treacherous double bend in the road. "Do you realise if the media finds out about this they'll be down here like an avalanche?"

"They cover every bad weather rescue."

"They do," Melanie agreed. "They also demand the identities of the people being rescued. They'll have a bean-feast when they discover the heir to the Gasquet throne is out there somewhere. And I dread to contemplate the king's reaction when he gets wind of this. Pardon my pun," she added when a gust of rising wind hit the car.

Taking a slow, deep breath, Monica shifted in her seat to glare at her friend. "I hope you are not laying this incident at my feet." Forcing her voice low and even, when she wanted to scream to the moon, she added sarcasm, saccharine-sweet, to her tone. "In case it escaped your notice, Henri is not a child in need of direction. He's an adult and as such is fully responsible for his own actions. So cut the whining."

In spite of her earlier retaliation, the full weight of Melanie's words weighed heavily on Monica's shoulders and guilt gnawed at her conscience. Had the stupid man ignored the storm warnings because of their altercation earlier that afternoon? Melanie wasn't so far off the mark with her accusation. Monica had been dialling the holiday company when her friend stomped into her home.

Running away, Melanie had accused. Henri didn't run away from anything. She already knew Henri never skirted 'round an issue. He homed in on the issue at hand. He preferred to tackle a problem directly. Hadn't he done just that with her today?

In essence, he'd told her she wasn't good enough to become a royal bride. And she'd had plenty of time to weigh his words to decide he was right. After all, hadn't she spent most of her life in the shadows in a futile attempt to avoid being hurt?

A coward. The self-accusation ringing in her head added fuel to his words. The memory of a radio news-clip she'd heard before Melanie's arrival, about some famous film star, came back to her. How had the woman managed to work in the full glare of media for several years' attention and still hide her true identity from them? True, after much media speculation, the film star in question had phoned the studio and come out, revealing she was the daughter of a former president of America. And the resulting furore simply added to Monica's own determination to run away, yet again.

But no more.

She straightened in her seat as the farmhouse came into view. A crowd of people hovered around the back door, all suited-up to withstand the approaching blizzard conditions. As if to confirm her thoughts, a gust of wind rocked the car when it came to a halt a few feet away from the crowd.

Liam strode to the driver's door and pulled it open. "I've contacted the police and we've decided to start with local help before calling in the official rescue teams."

"Isn't that a risk?" Melanie climbed out of the car and caught hold of her husband's arm to steady herself against another gust of wind.

Taking his wife's arm, Liam raised his voice to be heard. "If we leave it any longer, he could die from exposure, especially if he's hurt."

Goodness only knew that too few people survived the first fifteen minutes if buried in snow, and if Henri had taken a tumble, the wind and drifting snow reduced his chances dramatically, Monica thought, listening in to their conversation.

"Give us a minute to tog up and we'll join you," Melanie said.

"No, you have to stay at home." Before Monica's friend could protest, Liam held up his hand and looked across at Monica then back at Melanie. "No, darling. You must stay with Jonathon and monitor the phone. Monica…" Letting go of his wife, Liam then strode round the car and took Monica's arm. "You will come with us."

With a silent nod, she stepped back and as quickly as the wind allowed, headed towards the barn loft to change. The team of volunteers wouldn't know why Liam insisted she join them, and some probably objected, but she knew why, and was thankful that in some small way she might prove pivotal in Henri's rescue.

"Monica!"

His voice, weaker this time, stopped her halfway to the rooms above the barns.

"Monica…"

She whirled 'round and shouted for Liam. "Up the hill track. Don't waste time going around the lake."

The scene she'd been unable to make sense of weeks earlier, when she watched it in the fire, came back to her now — fully formed, sharp in every detail, and completely familiar to her. Why he'd headed in the direction of one of her favourite spots, she didn't know, but she did know without doubt almost exactly where they'd find Henri: at a spot where the ground levelled after a steep incline up the hill. To begin with the path climbed steadily, meandering through the trees, and then the climb became steeper, the path narrower, the tree-line thinning away to almost nothing. When riding for pleasure, as she usually did, it took up to and sometimes more than an hour to reach the level piece of ground bordered on one side with steep, dark grey outcrops of rock.

Tonight, if Henri had made it that far...? She shuddered to think how long it would take.

For a shimmering second Liam stared at her then spun on his heels. She dashed indoors to change. She heard him shouting out directions.

And hoped they'd be in time.

Five

February 11

Monica ignored the papers strewn across her makeshift desk in Henri's room. He'd been in a bad way when they found him, located exactly where she'd suggested, curled up against Raven. The horse had protected his rider from the worst of the drifting snow and by sharing his body warmth had given everyone more time to find the prince.

The rescuers' combined efforts soon had Henri strapped to a makeshift stretcher and carried back to the farm.

The local doctor, one of the volunteers, had then whisked him to hospital to operate on his broken arm, with the pronouncement, "He's a lucky man. But for the horse shielding him from the elements, we may not have found such a happy outcome."

"That's unlike Henri," the king had said over the phone when they 'fessed up to the incident. The fact that he added little else surprised everyone.

"Well!" Melanie had heaved a sigh of relief when Liam ended the call. "That went better than expected."

"It did." Liam's pensive tone and glance in her direction had Monica squirming in her chair. "I wonder…"

"What?" Melanie shot up in her chair. "What?"

When Liam just grinned at her, she rose and stomped off to the kitchen to refill her coffee cup.

Something in Liam's tone had sent a frisson of anxiety coursing through Monica's blood. Much as she yearned to know what Liam wondered, she refrained from asking him. One, from fear she may not like the answer, and then again, for some reason she got the impression Liam wanted her to ask and she refused to give him the satisfaction of denying her curiosity.

Now, her gaze homed in on the pot of cheerful early daffodils sitting on the window-sill. *Springtime,* she thought. *Well, not quite.* With three days left until Valentine's Day, winter still had enough clout to pitch them all back into blizzard conditions. Thankfully, the weatherman promised bright, cold, sunny days running up to and including Valentine's Day itself.

A sound from the bed had her swivelling in her chair to discover Henri's eyes watching her.

"Can I get you anything?" she asked, rising to sit on the edge of his bed. She treasured the quiet time she'd spent with him, both while he slept and when he woke.

He'd talked a little of his life as the heir to his father's throne. The duties and expectations he'd been tutored to accept almost as soon as he could toddle. Yes, he'd told her, he did have a family life but not to the same extent as his brothers.

He'd admitted that sometimes the enormity of his future commitments overwhelmed him, and in those darker moments he saddled up and rode to a favourite spot of his to think and relax. When he described the rock pool, the high cliffs to one side and the expansive view of steep mountains and deep valley on the other, she'd laughed. Her favourite spot might lack the towering mountains of his country, but, she told him on one occasion, he could have been describing the spot she always sought in times of emotional turmoil.

"In fact," she'd added, "we think that's where you were heading when you took that tumble."

She'd laughed at his derisive response. "Since I've never been there, and I certainly don't remember you telling me about it, how would I know it was there or how to reach it?"

"Why did you saddle up Raven and not Demon as usual?" she'd come back with.

"I don't know. It was not a deliberate choice on my part," he admitted.

"Well, whatever your reason, Raven would take you there blindfolded."

"He didn't this time," Henri shot back.

"True," she agreed. "The difference being, I have never attempted to ride there with an imminent blizzard forecast."

Henri's silence confirmed her barb had reached its mark.

"No, there's nothing I need," he said now in answer to her question. "I feel a fool lying here when there's nothing wrong with me."

"Well, a broken arm certainly wouldn't keep you off your feet normally, but the doctor wanted to keep an eye on you to make sure you didn't develop pneumonia or some such problem. You were lucky Raven didn't try to make his way home without you." She couldn't prevent the hitch in her voice and looked away. The nodding daffodils mocked her melancholy. "Your father is sending his plane for you tomorrow." She couldn't look at him, couldn't reveal her misery.

"Then he's wasting his time. I have no intention of returning home before your Valentine shindig. Is that the right word?"

The warmth of his hand on her elbow crept through the material of her shirt. His tug on her arm persuaded her to look 'round.

"I'm not going home before then," he said. "We have to talk and you have too much to do right now." He indicated the scatter of papers that had spread to his bed. "Indeed, I am sure there must be something I can do to help. Phone calls, crossing items off your many lists. Tell me what I can do to help."

"I couldn't ask you to do that." Monica spluttered.

"Why not? You let Liam help, why not me? Consider it a kindness."

"What?"

"I'll die of boredom instead of hypothermia if I don't have something to do." His grin lit up his face and wrapped another chain round her heart.

She thought of half a dozen excellent reasons for not helping him, but one look at Henri's face had her buttoning her lips. She nodded, and watched him rearrange his pillows and make himself comfortable. She knew better than to offer help. The last time she did, he'd blasted her for fussing too much. With an effort she marshalled her thoughts and itemised the most pressing stuff on her list, and with Henri's help set to work.

🐎

February 14

"I'm surprised you have any energy left for the dance tonight." Favouring his injured arm, Henri stood in front of the blazing fire in the sitting room. "Yesterday you cleared and cleaned out the training ring." He thought of the indoor shed they used in winter for their schooling and training. "Today you've run yourself ragged catering for the various children's parties and games. Melanie said you started at six o'clock this morning." Glancing at his watch, he sighed. "You've been on your feet for twelve hours."

"So?"

"Don't you ever get tired?"

More so than you'll ever know, Monica thought, and carried a tray of drinks across the room so it joined the others on the sideboard for gathering family and friends to enjoy before joining other arrivals in the arena for the evening dance held for adults only.

"It's only once a year," she offered.

He caught her arm. Waited until she looked up at him. "We need to talk; you know that, don't you?"

"There's nothing more to say. You made yourself very clear on the afternoon of your accident." She tugged her arm free and made a show of arranging the additional bottles. "And I still have a hundred things to do before—"

"I did nothing more than make an idiot of myself," Henri interrupted.

"Leave it. Just leave it," she pleaded.

After his mysterious disappearance for most of the day two days prior, Melanie had confirmed just hours ago that Henri was flying home permanently the day after the dance, and this time when Monica announced her intention to go on holiday at the end of the week, her friend had not interfered.

The diminishing sound of children's voices alerted her to the need to change. Instead, she lingered at the bar and, keeping her back to Henri, asked the question that had bothered her for days. "Tell me something."

"What?"

She heard the hesitancy in his voice.

"I know the locals treat you and Liam as one of their own."

"They don't know who we are, for sure."

"Of course they do! They read the papers, watch TV, and go online. They know. They simply have the courtesy and integrity not to blab to the media. As I say, they treat you as part of their community."

"So?" Henri conceded that Monica had a point. Perhaps he and Liam still had a tendency to stick their heads in the sand over some things, recognition by the locals being one of them.

"How do you cope with all the media hoopla? This place excluded, you are followed wherever you go, always the butt of a good story when the papers' sales drop. They intrude whenever they can, wherever they can. Doesn't it bother you?"

"Yes, it bothers me, but after a while..." He shrugged one shoulder. "I won't claim you become inured, because if you do you become careless, and you always have to be on the alert for the catch, the unintentional quote you give them that is often misrepresented."

"I can't imagine how you deal with it."

"It's a fact of my life, the same way your intuition and healing abilities are a fact of yours."

"That's my point." Something flickered in his eye; understanding perhaps, but that wasn't all. She wanted to see love and denied herself the chance to hope. He'd marry someone more sophisticated, someone from his own social sphere. As if to emphasise her disbelief in what she saw, she soldiered on. "When people learn about my abilities, they shy away. You did."

She shook her head when he began to deny it.

"Don't even try; you were out that door so fast you left burn marks in the carpet."

His heightened colour told her he remembered as clearly as she did his hasty retreat when she predicted his marriage and the birth of his first child.

"Will you give me the first dance?" Henri asked. "I gather from Melanie you usually give that one to James."

Her eyes clouded with grief. James had remained in Switzerland for a few more days after taking his wife to the clinic, then notified them he was going to tour 'round Europe for a few weeks before returning home. No one voiced the truth: he couldn't face coming to the dance so soon after losing his beloved wife.

Who could blame him?

Suddenly shy, she nodded and hoped Henri couldn't see her heart cartwheeling in her chest. She'd accept every crumb of his company he offered this evening, because tomorrow when he left she'd never see him again.

If he came over to visit Liam and Melanie in the future, she'd make sure to be away at the time.

Accepting that she could never have the man she loved as her husband, she saw no reason to inflict unnecessary pain to her heart for the rest of her life. Nor was she prepared to give up her share of the riding school simply because Henri might, only *might,* visit occasionally.

Two days ago, Henri had ordered the royal plane and flown home. After a quick word with his parents, he'd collected a small item from the palace vault and returned to the farmhouse the same day.

Now as he offered comfort for her grief for her friends, he brushed his lips over her hair and stroked his good hand soothingly over her back. Her perfume teased his nostrils. Subtle like the lady; full of mysteries, strong and yet never over-ostentatious. She had everything the wife of a ruler would need to hold her own against a sometimes intrusive world. All he had to do was persuade her, and that, he concluded with a grimace, would be no easy task.

And he could blame only himself. From the outset he'd set out to wrong-foot her and wondered whether, regardless of the chemistry flaring between them, he would win her love.

And he'd seen it in her eyes often enough, when she thought he wasn't looking, to be certain she did love him. Almost losing his life the night of the blizzard had convinced him of the stupidity of agreeing to an arranged marriage when the woman who owned his heart lived a few measly hours away by plane. He couldn't do it. Not now.

The satisfied smirk on his father's face when he revealed he'd ordered the pilot to log a return flight to Scotland gave him pause for thought at the time. And he wondered whether the canny old soul had had an ulterior motive when he sent his eldest son to Scotland for a recuperative holiday.

With a murmur, Monica lifted her head from his shoulder and stepped away. "I have to go and get ready."

"You're not going home, are you?"

She shook her head and pointed through the window towards the barn loft. "I stay there for the week running up to Valentine's Day, and tonight."

No wonder she hadn't commented on his card. He'd sent it to her home address. He hadn't signed it, but after they'd been working together this last week, she should know his writing well enough by now to recognise it on a card. He sighed. It would make tonight's plans less straightforward, but not scupper them completely. He caught her chin in his fingers, brushed his lips over hers, and then sang

"Save the Last Dance for Me" as she left the room.

First dance, last dance, and as many in between he could get away with, Henri thought with a satisfied smile, and headed for his bedroom to prepare for the evening's festivities.

His brother ambushed his attention before he'd taken a step. Liam nodded, crossed the room, poured himself a drink, then walked to stand looking out of the window.

With a shrug, Henri joined him. Together they stared out the window at the six-foot-high, gold-coloured Cupid statues on each side of the closed arena doors. "If I didn't know better, I'd say those Cupid statues came from the palace."

"You're right, they did," Liam confirmed.

"Why won't they let us help them?" Did his voice really sound as whiny to Liam as it did in his head, Henri wondered, and glowered at the building declared out of bounds to all by Monica and Melanie for the last twenty-four hours.

"Apparently they do this every year. You can imagine how I felt on the fifteenth, last year, when Melanie told me she was two months pregnant. I mean, she'd have had to climb ladders, lift all the decorations they pinned to the ceiling, and I didn't dare try to remember what else she'd done that I'd have banned if I'd known."

"So they decorate the place?"

"Absolutely. Hearts, bows and arrows, little Cupids, medium Cupids, and now, thanks to Mother, two hulking great Cupids, which, thankfully, are outside so I can deal with them."

"I had no idea Valentine's Day was so big here."

"It is generally big in this country," Liam agreed, "but here we also use it as a way of thanking everyone who keeps the school going with their help and support during the year."

"The children certainly had a ball. If I'd been running after them all day, I'd be too shattered by now to even think of dancing, let alone handling the finishing touches those two maintain they are dealing with. Those women could teach some members of the palace staff a thing or two."

Henri expected Liam to join in his laughter and swung round to perceive his brother's serious expression. "What?" He shifted from one foot to the other.

"You're in love with her, aren't you?"

Why deny the obvious, Henri thought with a shrug. "Yes."

"Have you told her?"

"No—"

"You'll lose her if you're not careful."

Henri studied his brother's face for a sign of mirth and found none. "And you say this, why?"

"You saw the brochures on her table when we went over to her place this morning. For all her impression of invulnerability, Monica expects rejection like most people anticipate the sunrise every morning."

"But why? She's a strong and independent woman; why would she assume I'd reject her?" He felt the heat in his face and groaned. "Stupid question."

"When Monica loves, she gives everything she has. She has learned too often that people turn away from her when they discover her gift." Liam paused, looked him in the eye, and moved in closer. "Like you did."

"What are you saying?" Bewildered, Henri stepped sideways, cast a glance over his shoulder at the arena, then crossed the room to get a drink.

"When you came off your horse, did you call out for her?"

With his whiskey glass raised halfway to his lips, Henri paused, thought back, then nodded. "I believe I did," he admitted, then took a gulp of amber liquid. He had called out for her. Fear of never seeing her again had wrenched the call through his lips, as did his regrets for never declaring his love for her. And still he had not.

"Don't be daft." Henri tried to laugh off Liam's claim and knew he lied to himself. "I believe I called for her twice," he challenged.

"And twice she heard you. Once in Melanie's car, and again, a matter of ten minutes or so later, when I sent her to kit up for our search and rescue mission. After all, no one else would know where to start looking. A couple of men in the team wanted to go 'round the lake but Monica held her ground and guided us straight to you."

"How did she know where to look?" Henri refilled his glass and shot a sceptical glance in his brother's direction.

"Ah!" Liam sighed. "Bring me a drink. I'm going to need it by the time I've finished explaining this."

Henri crossed the room, handed the glass to Liam, and looked down at the barn. He'd scoffed at Monica the night Melanie asked him to take the papers over to Monica, and how she'd started talking while staring at the orange flames of her open fire. And how it had ended with him accusing her of being an opportunistic optimist before he stormed out of her house

"According to Melanie," Liam began, "Monica has seen images in flames since before she started school. It is not for me to go into detail. All I'll say is that something happened in her first term and from that moment on, all her friends ridiculed and bullied her right through her school years. As if that wasn't bad enough, both her parents pretty much did the same to her."

"Melanie knows about all this?" Henri shook his head as remorse warred with disbelief.

With a single nod of his head Liam continued. "The first snow of the winter fell in early November." He cast a level look in Henri's direction. "Normally it would be a dusting, but this was a long and heavy snowstorm with gale-force winds banking the snow up against the hills and filling the gullies. Roads were blocked and power lines broke like matchsticks.

"That evening, soon after the snow began falling, Monica phoned Melanie and told her she'd heard a man's voice, and no, she didn't recognise it. She did say it wasn't a local."

"How could she claim that?" Henri wanted to dismiss Liam's account out of hand and couldn't quite manage it. "Go on," he added.

"By the accent. It wasn't Scottish, and to quote Monica's description here, she described it as *'Too refined.'*" He paused. "While all this was happening to Monica, you were back at home, all but killing yourself trying to fulfil the king's duties as well as your own."

"So?"

"She recognised the area she was seeing, and almost contacted the police and search and rescue teams."

Troubled by the image of Monica as she stared at her fire and described his sitting room in his private suite in the palace to perfection, Henri failed to curb the snap in his voice. "Almost? What stopped her?"

"She told Melanie that 'it hadn't happened yet.' And when you first called out to Monica for help, she recognised your voice as the one she heard way back in November." Before he could interrupt Liam continued. "After you were taken to the hospital, Melanie asked her why she hadn't recognised your voice when you first arrived."

"And?"

"It was the terror in your voice, both when she heard it back in November and again when you decided to ignore the weather warning that had been given out and gone riding."

Henri wanted to deny it, to disbelieve, and couldn't. In his gut he knew Liam spoke the truth, and that he was still talking.

"—again, she saw the scene in the flames and nearly called the police."

"And when did she tell Melanie all this?" Henri wanted to deny it, to disbelieve, and couldn't. In his gut he knew Liam spoke the truth.

"I told you, last November, minutes after she experienced her vision in the flames, she rang Melanie and asked whether she should call the police or not.

"Until she guided us straight to you, I'd not seen evidence of her ability to find people in a storm, but on the way back when we were carrying you to the farmhouse and again at the hospital, several people came up to us and shared stories about the individuals they knew that Monica had helped before."

"And they accept this — this gift without prejudice? I find that hard to believe."

"They do," Liam stated firmly. "At first I doubted, as you do now, but have heard too many tales and seen too much evidence to back them up not to believe in her abilities. It is something you would do well to consider before this night is over."

Hadn't he stormed out of her house the night she told him he'd marry and be bouncing his first child on his knee within a year?

"So she can predict things for others…what about herself?"

Liam shook his head. "She maintains it never works like that. And…" He paused, topped up his drink. "I've heard similar cases where the intuitive or psychic can help others, but rarely themselves."

"Why not?"

Liam shook his head. "You'd have to ask her."

Had she predicted his marriage as a form of manipulation? Or had she simply seen him married but not known to whom? He stared at the closed arena doors, half hoping she'd come through them and look up. At that moment, he wished he had the power to distract her from whatever she was doing inside the building and "call" her out to him.

"The women normally use the kitchen and restrooms over there to dress." Liam interrupted his thoughts. "So I suggest you head on upstairs and get ready."

Several people had warned Henri the dance usually went on into the wee small hours of the morning, and he decided to take his brother's advice. He'd adapted to the cast on his broken arm, but the weariness that still plagued him from early evening on bothered him. Especially tonight, when he wanted to spend most of it with Monica safely wrapped in his arms.

🐎

"I hope your brother knows what he's doing." Contrary to Liam's prediction, his wife followed him into their room soon after he arrived there and began preparing for the dance. Now she picked up her bottle of perfume from the dresser and spritzed herself.

"They're both adults. Don't interfere," Liam growled from the bathroom.

"The last time you mentioned that, Henri nearly died out in the snow." The perfume bottle hit the dresser's surface with a snap. "This time he could end up with a broken heart. Why can't the fool tell her he loves her?" She glanced in the mirror, starting to apply her lip gloss, when her husband's troubled tone stopped her.

"Because—" Liam entered their bedroom, a troubled look on his face. "—I'm not sure he knows how to. It is not easy for Henri to show or admit to deep personal emotions. Over the years they got buried under a mountain of royal protocol. It began before he was old enough to understand what was happening, because he was learning to meet the expectations of his position."

"How can he not know whether he's in love with Monica? You only have to look at the goofy expression on his face when he looks at her to see he's head-over-heels in love with her."

"Did I look at you like that?" Liam's feral grin coaxed a laugh from his wife.

"No, you did not." Her attempt at hauteur failed, sabotaged by another laugh. "You looked hungry."

"That's because I was." Like one of Cupid's arrows, Liam's simple statement shot straight to her heart.

"You do know she's booked a month's holiday starting at the end of this week, don't you?"

"I do, and so does my brother."

"Oh!" Wrong-footed by this admission, Melanie wasn't sure how to respond. "Does he know where she's going?" she asked after a pause.

"He does."

"He does? How did he find out? She won't tell me." Pouting, Melanie picked up the diamond bracelet Liam had given her immediately after Jonathon's birth and held it out for him to fasten for her.

"Remember when Monica asked me to collect those files for her this morning?"

Melanie nodded. They'd been up to their ears in children's games.

"Henri came with me and we saw the papers on her tabletop. Henri went through them very carefully."

"That was a bit underhanded, wasn't it?"

"Perhaps. You know what they say. 'All is fair in love and war.'"

"I can't say I've ever thought of their relationship as war — precisely," Melanie mused.

"Oh, my dear, what's happened to your powers of observation? From the moment Henri laid eyes on her when she walked into the room before Christmas, he declared war. That is so unlike my phlegmatic brother, I nearly choked with laughter. It took me all my time to keep a straight face."

"You sneaky son of a gun! You might have told me." Melanie stood, gave her image one last stare then turned into her husband's arms. "I'll forgive you if you kiss me senseless."

"How cruel you are when you know your guests are arriving as we speak. And later, my dear—" He kissed her nose. "—you'll pay for teasing me."

"Promises, promises," she said, laughing, and let him chase her down the stairs.

Six

February 14

The bell peeled.

"Will you get that?" Wishing the night away before it began, Melanie stepped aside when they reached the hallway and motioned towards the front door.

Liam strode across the hall, swung the door open, and gaped. "What? When? How?"

Simeon Theo Gasquet stepped into the hall, shoved a finger beneath his brother's chin, and closed his gaping mouth. "We were invited." Smiling over Liam's shoulder, Simeon winked at his sister-in-law.

Sacha Mathieu Gasquet followed his twin into the house. "As soon as we received Melanie's invitation this afternoon. And the how must surely be obvious to you. By jet, of course."

Once the hugs were over, Liam peered into the darkness beyond the open door. "Where're the parents? Don't tell me they're not here."

"They are not here," Simeon confirmed. "Where's Henri?"

"Here."

Everyone looked up when his voice came from the top of the stairs.

"It's good to see you both." Henri hurried down to join his younger brothers. His glance fell on Melanie's shining face, her eyes alight with joy. "This is your doing, isn't it?"

"Partly," Melanie agreed, and stepped into Simeon's embrace before turning to his twin.

"I'm sorry to disturb you." From the open kitchen door at the far end of the hallway, Rosie's unsure voice broke up the greeting, and Melanie moved across to her.

"What's the matter?"

"Nothing precisely," Rosie answered, but her gaze focussed on someone behind Melanie. Melanie swung 'round to see the same love-struck expression on Sacha's face.

"I take it those are the Gaquet twins?" Awe transformed Rosie's voice into a husky whisper. Of its own volition, her hand crept up to cover her heart. "It's not fair." She forced herself to look at Melanie. "They're like two peas in a pod, and yet..." she hesitated, "they're completely different."

Amazed, Melanie looked back at her latest arrivals. Not many people could accurately identify the twins when they were in the same room, and yet at a first glance here was Rosie claiming they were 'completely different.' "Different? How?"

"The way they stand, and..." Rosie paused again, "and hold their heads when they are relaxed."

Melanie understood, but failed to work out how her friend was aware of them in a matter of seconds. "That's not much to go on," she challenged. "Certainly not enough to recognise the difference if you saw them on their own."

"No, perhaps not, but the difference is there, if indefinable." Caution laced her voice now as she became aware that everyone had turned toward her, and were listening. "I mean, they are both tall, but there is a difference in the angle of their shoulders."

"That could be because Simeon is wearing a designer suit and so is Sacha, but from the look of him, he might as well be wearing jeans and a T-shirt." Liam crossed the floor to stand beside Melanie.

"Well, there you are." At Rosie's satisfied response, both twins joined Liam, and both had the same similar satisfied sparkle in their eyes.

"I don't follow you." Henri's cool tone drew a disgusted snort from his youngest siblings.

"Knock it off, Henri. We want to know how Rosie would recognise us even if she met us when we were on our own." Instead of turning to face his brother, Sacha reached out for Rosie's hand and offered her a smile of encouragement. "What's the difference? For you are the only person I know who has made such a claim within seconds of seeing us. Even some of our closest friends have difficulty telling us apart when we're in the same room."

Simeon, his face grim now, nodded his agreement. "I am as curious as Sacha to learn more, for if you are telling the truth, you will be unique in your claim."

"It is as I said and Liam agreed with me. It is the way you carry yourselves. You could both wear the same clothes, but you, Simeon, are more contained within yourself, while Sacha is full of mischief."

Liam broke the stunned silence filling the hallway. "How many times have our parents voiced those same words, from when you were both little kids to the last time I was home?"

"Because you told her?" Simeon's eyes narrowed when Liam shook his head. "Then she overheard you telling Melanie."

Again Liam shook his head. "You know very well Melanie has always struggled to tell you two apart.

It was one of your greatest challenges to confuse her when she lived at the palace as part of the security detail. And you were successful for years."

Rosie stood tall and glared at Simeon. "No one, but no one calls me a liar and gets away with it." Snatching her hand out of Sacha's grip, she marched across the hall and wrenched open a door to reveal a full-length mirror fixed to the other side. "Both of you come over here."

The snap in her voice amazed Melanie. Never had she heard Rosie raise her voice to anyone in all the years she'd known her.

Sacha grinned, and Simeon scowled, but both of them crossed to stand in front of the mirror.

"Look at yourself, Simeon. You look as though you're about to enter a boardroom to deal with a tough negotiation, instead of arriving to participate in a Valentine's Day party with family." She failed to hide her grin while Simeon's scowl darkened. "As for you, Sacha," and she grinned, then cursed silently when heat bloomed in her cheeks. "If I didn't know you are a European Royal, whose family history disappears back to ancient times, I'd assume you were Irish through and through."

The twins looked from the mirror to each other then laughed.

"You can't deny it, bro. She's clocked us good and proper. Isn't that what you Brits say?" Sacha turned to Melanie to discover she was creased over with laughter.

When she managed to stop laughing, Melanie put her hand on Rosie's shoulder. "I'm not sorry we were distracted, but you came to find me for a reason. Is there a problem in the arena?" she asked, forcing her attention back to the final and biggest event of the day.

"It's Monica."

"Monica?" Henri was beside them before Melanie saw him move. "Is she all right?"

"She's fine." Rosie looked from one brother to the other and straightened. "She asked me to send for you, Melanie." Her request given, Rosie inhaled deeply, cast one more glance in Sacha's direction, and scuttled from the hall.

Well, well, Melanie thought. *Two down, no, make that one-and-a-half so far...* Was another unsuspecting Gasquet about to meet his match?

"Excuse me, gentlemen," she said and laid a restraining hand on Henri's arm when he made to follow her.

🐎

For a full minute, torn between his need to go to Monica and enjoying the unexpected arrival of his brothers, Henri stood rooted to the spot where Melanie had left him.

He hadn't seen the twins since before Christmas, and the sight of Simeon and Sacha here in the farmhouse, bringing the four of them together again, set emotions churning in his chest. *Family matters,* he thought. He knew that, he told himself, as first Simeon then Sacha clamped him in effusive hugs. But tonight, something more shimmered in the air around them.

"He's got it bad." Simeon's chuckle brought him out of his stasis.

My brother may joke, but many a truth has been spoken in jest before now, or so the saying goes, Henri mused, and rejoined his family.

"I can understand what drew you to this place."

Simeon's serious tone caught Henri's attention. "And?"

"There's a warmth about it and I don't mean physical." He gave a shudder. "It's cold outside, yes,

I know that, but it's deeper. The place breathes it."
With a dismissive wave of his hand, Simeon moved
across the hall to peer into the sitting room. "It's the
same in here. Even in the darkness, I felt something
as we approached the farmhouse. I can't explain it."

He didn't need to, Henri thought, and on catch-
ing Liam's gaze knew he understood, too.

"Homey?" Sacha asked, not quite disguising the
sarcasm in his voice.

"Don't knock it, bro," Simeon said. "We have a
good home, but this is—" He hesitated. "—more
earthy. More real."

"Careful, twin, you're beginning to wax lyrical. If
you're not careful, you'll be the next to fall in love.
With two down, we need to stick together." Sacha
spied the drinks on the other side of the room and
made a beeline for them. It surprised Henri to see
his brother select a ginger ale and sip.

The conversation drifted around him while his
thoughts roamed. So much hung on the outcome
tonight. The arrival of his brothers upped the ante.
If Monica turned him down... He couldn't even bear
to finish the thought.

Simeon came to stand beside him, sharing a
companionable silence for a while. "Tell me about
her."

Henri sighed and wondered how you described
the other half of yourself. How could he verbalise
that without Monica at his side, he'd only be half a
person? Only be half the king he could be if she
didn't stand beside him? Simeon would think he'd
lost his marbles.

"There comes a time in your life when it changes
in a second. One minute you're travelling life's path,
carefree..."

"You've never been carefree," Simeon interrupted with an understanding murmur. "Go on."

"I won't say I didn't notice her when she came over for Melanie and Liam's renewal of their marriage vows. I did."

"We noticed."

Henri grinned at Simeon's verbal dig now. The twins had been at the receiving end of his temper a time or two and knew, while hot and hard at the time, he always apologised, if need be, before long. "I'd no sooner arrived here than I found out she'd been behind the idea of getting me to Scotland. I was so furious." With a rueful grin, he shrugged and let the rest hang in the air, while at the same time wondering how he'd been stupid enough to think letting his parents choose his bride would work.

"And did she forgive you?"

"By mutual consent we kept our distance from one another."

"Sparring partners before the battle," Simeon muttered. "How like you."

"What does that mean?" Henri snapped, irritated by Simeon's less-than-subtle reproof.

"It means, Henri, that true to condition, you always put others before yourself, whether they are family, friends, or matters of state. Back home we make allowances for the fact that you have been schooled to take over from our father one day, but this Monica, how can she understand that you stand back because..." Simeon's voice trailed away.

"Don't stop now; you're just getting to the interesting part." Temper joined his apprehension about how the evening would end and combined into a dark bubbling brew of emotions. He stuffed his fists into his pockets before they had a chance to connect with his brother's chin. Truth, he discovered, when uttered by someone else, had a nasty habit of cutting through all his excuses with the ease of a hot knife through butter. The knowledge did not sit well in his conscience.

"Oh, come on, Henri, Simeon's right." Sacha joined them where they stood in front of the darkened window. "How can the woman understand your deep-seated sense of responsibility? She has no conception of your royal duties. I bet you've never talked about them. Melanie may have, I'll grant you that, but it's not the same."

His certainty that he and Monica could have a life together evaporated. The twins were right. How could he expect Monica, independent, outdoor-loving Monica, to give up all this and her freedom to become his wife and be sucked in by the demands of his country and the palace? He had to be mad.

He'd thought the time they'd spent together after his return from hospital had been enough to bring them together. Now, listening to his brothers, he knew how wrong — how unreasonable — he'd been to even contemplate asking her to share the restrictions of his preordained life

He'd go in there tonight and have every possible dance with her that he could wangle. He fingered the ring box in his pocket. And tomorrow he'd return home. Alone.

"You're right," he said, not sure whether it was his voice or his heart that broke. "Asking her to share such a life as mine is totally selfish."

"More like that of a coward," Sacha and Simeon said together.

Liam joined them, his brow furrowed. "What is this? Is this how you intend to run the country in the future?"

"What are you talking about?"

Liam, his nose all but pressed against Henri's, exploded. "When you are king, are you going to run at the first sign of trouble? Are you going to turn tail and hide when you are too afraid to fight for your heart's desire? I'm disappointed in you, Henri." With that Liam spun on his heel and stalked from the room.

After a moment's ear-splitting silence, Simeon and Sacha followed.

"Give him time." Sacha leaned down to his dance partner and whispered. "He's got a lot to think about, and Henri, when faced with a dilemma, always takes his time."

"He's going home with you tomorrow, isn't he?" Monica swallowed the tears clogging her throat.

"I don't know, and I don't think he does either."

"Then why isn't he here?"

"I'm afraid it's partly my fault and partly Simeon's," Sacha admitted.

"How can you be responsible? He's been moody for days."

"Henri is many things, Monica, but moody is not one of them."

When she snorted, Sacha shook her gently by the shoulder and still managed not to miss a dance beat.

"It's a twin thing. Most of our life, at least since we understood the difference between our choices for the future and Henri's, it's been our life's aim to wind him up a bit. We were doing that earlier, only it didn't go the way we intended. Just the opposite, in fact!" Sacha ended on a sigh, and pulling Monica closer, whirled her across the dance floor.

Monica danced with every man in the room, some of them twice. Just a pity Henri wasn't one of them. He was the only man she wanted to dance with. The thought of the holiday booking she'd confirmed that afternoon didn't compensate for Henri's absence or the underlying message behind his non-appearance, but it did strengthen her spine sufficiently to get her through what was turning out to be a nightmare of an evening.

For the last two days, with Henri at the forefront of her mind, Monica had lovingly hung Cupid bows all over the ceiling, intermingled with red hearts and golden arrows. She'd emptied every florist within a twenty-mile radius of every red flower and plant they could lay their hands on and set them 'round the room.

She'd pestered the caterers to include a schmaltzy quantity of Valentine-themed foods of every kind. They'd even created red pastry. She noted not many people had gone for the flaky hearts and wasn't sure she could blame them.

At personal expense, she'd ordered reams of red velvet and draped the walls with it, and decorated the velvet with golden stars and more hearts and Cupid bows.

Everyone who'd come told her they were the best decorations they'd ever seen at the farm, and over the years she and Melanie had offered plenty of variations.

Every final touch she'd put into this year's Valentine dance was prompted by her love for Henri, and the man hadn't had the decency to turn up.

"Yes, he has." Sacha laughed.

"What?" Bewildered, Monica missed a step as she tried to make sense of her partner's words.

"He's turned up." Sacha swung her round and there, framed by the open doorway, was Henri, his eyes searching the room. Obviously she'd spoken her thoughts aloud, and she blushed, wondering just how many of them she'd verbalised. One look at her dance partner's face told her: more than she'd intended.

Before she knew what Sacha was up to, Monica

found herself waltzed across the floor and standing in front of the man she loved.

Unaware of Sacha's signal to the band, she stepped into Henri's arms and sighed when he pulled her firmly against his chest and began to dance. His heart was beating as fast as hers. The warmth of his breath fanned her hair away from her eyes. The smile she was sure lit her face started in her heart. If this was all she'd have of him, she'd treasure every millisecond of it so she could take it out and remember it in the future, long after Henri had returned to his own country and his royal duties.

The warmth of his hand on her back spelled safety. His arms cradled her, even while dancing. Her dislike of dance partners holding her so firmly normally shattered her nerves. Not when he danced her out of the arena and into the night. Not when Henri's arms, in spite of the solid cast on one of them, offered safety, security, and a sense of belonging. She only wished it could last beyond tonight.

Starlight replaced the overhead lights in the arena and the sighing wind orchestrated the waving branches overhead.

And then everything vanished, and the only thing in the world that mattered was Henri's lips on hers. Feasting, demanding, taking.

She relished the feast, offered more, and gave wantonly. Whatever he offered this night, she'd accept, she promised herself.

Whatever.

His hands cupped her face, angled it to better taste her. She opened for him and tasted the whiskey on his tongue, smelled the woodsy cologne he favoured, and fisted her fingers in his hair to pull him closer.

He pulled her closer, too, allowing her hair to trail through his fingers. The heat scorched down her neck as his hand moved, followed by his lips. When he found the pulse point at the base of her throat, she swore she heard bells ringing.

Her hands moved from Henri's hair to roam over his back. Raking, pulling, pushing. Emotions she never suspected herself capable of coursed through her. While Henri's lips moved on down from her throat, her hand began tugging his shirt free.

Something changed. Cool wind blew over heated skin, Henri's hands dropped away, fisted and disappeared into his pockets. And so far he'd not spoken one single word. Ready to flee, she straightened her spine, looked into his face, and stepped back in shock.

Love!

Lit by the illumination spilling from the arena, she saw it clearly; love shone from his eyes. Not lust. *That* she'd expected after their heated exchange at the lake.

He took one of her hands in his and pulled her up against him again, his other hand stroking through her hair, soothing this time, not arousing. "Will you come with me?"

Without a backward glance at the arena, Monica nodded and followed Henri into the farmhouse.

"Will you come to my room?" he asked. "We won't be interrupted and there are things I have to tell you." He paused. "Things I want to ask you."

Again she nodded and let him lead the way upstairs. Once in his room, Henri shut the door behind them with what seemed like a definitive click. When he pulled her into his arms, she responded to his hard and thorough kiss, protesting when he stepped away, and led her to a chair near the window. Beyond the dark, music from the arena, muffled by the glass, managed to infiltrate the room. With an irritated flick, Henri pulled the curtains closed.

"Just you and me, Monica."

He dropped into the chair facing her and leaned forward, his elbows on his thighs, his hands, fingers linked, between his knees.

Seven

February 14

He yearned to touch her, to run his fingers down her pale cheek. He wanted, hoped, to remove the anxiety lurking in her eyes. He wanted to ask a question he suspected she couldn't answer. He leaned forward, caught hold of her hand again. He needed the connection, and watched his thumb trace lines across the back of her hand.

Monica! He let her name swirl inside his head. How had the woman become a magnet for his heart? The gentle tug of her hand recalled him from his fantasies.

He cleared his throat. "Do you remember the evening I visited your flat?"

She nodded. He watched her eyes darken and knew she remembered his rebuff. Keeping her hand in his, he carried on, praying that by pursuing his instinct he wouldn't ruin things.

"I watched you staring into the flames that night and something fell into place within me."

Her face crumpled and she pulled her hand free. "Don't I know it?"

When tears shimmered in her eyes he rose and brushed them away with his thumb. "Hear me out, please." He'd get down on his knees and beg if he had to.

She'd risen, too, and stood glaring at him. "You walked, Henri. I didn't mean to let you in, but I did. I shared a side of me only my trusted friends understand, and you walked. That's what fell into place for you." She swung away from him, her arms wrapped around her body, her shoulders hunched.

"I can't deny it," Henri admitted. "But later, when I let myself think about it, it fell into place. It felt right."

"Right?" She raised her face to his and he saw hope.

Taking her hand yet again, he persuaded her back into the chair and knelt in front of her. "Will you answer one question for me?"

Hesitantly she nodded.

"You said you saw me with my child on my knee and it would happen within the next twelve months. Did you see the mother of my child?"

"No."

"Why was that?" A smile that started in his heart spread out until it almost split his face in two.

"I don't know."

"Yes, you do." He cupped her chin between forefinger and thumb. "Yes, you do," he said again.

"Knowing and hoping are two different things, Henri." Her voice quavered.

"You hoped, even then, it could be you?" His heart threatened to burst with joy when she nodded, her eyes turning shy.

"Even when I was so…"

"'Downright unpleasant' is what you are searching for, I think," she prompted when his words ran out.

He laughed and pulled her into his arms. "You captured my heart when I saw you walk down the aisle in front of Melanie."

"For me, it was when we joined Liam and

Melanie on the dance floor. I noticed you in the cathedral, of course I did. But there you were part of all the pomp and circumstance that is your life; on the dance floor you were just a man." She looked up, laughter sparkling in her eyes. "If you know what I mean."

"I do," he said seriously. "And it is why we need to talk, really talk without interruption."

He should let her go again; instead he wrapped her in his arms more firmly. "As you have just said, my life is one surrounded with pomp and circumstance. Rituals and routines. It is lived in the spotlight more often than even I like. I love you enough to let you go if you think you cannot live that kind of life with me.

"It means giving up your place here, the people you love and a lifestyle that is what you are. It means becoming a member of my family, who, in part, is owned by our people. You will have to give up a lot if you agree to marry me."

"Marry!"

"Of course marry. What else do you suppose I am talking about?" Thoroughly disconcerted by her query, he pushed away from her and stared into her startled face.

"Is that a request or a demand, Your Highness?"

At her teasing tone, he released a breath he hadn't known was trapped in his throat.

"Tell me about your life, the life you want me to share."

Disappointment seared through his chest at her evasion. He settled down in the chair she'd vacated, pulled her onto his knee, and told her everything about his life as the heir to a royal throne.

Some of it Monica knew from Melanie, but listening to Henri, to the inflections in his voice, she learned so much more. He took his destiny seriously, and appeared never to have questioned it, never rebelled from the mantle of responsibility he would inherit one day.

She knew he had a sense of humour from watching the brothers together, both in their own country and tonight for the brief time Henri had been in the converted ballroom. And he both adored and respected his parents. Not an easy accomplishment, when those parents were also wrapped up in official duties and circumstance and were surrounded by others, all with their own agendas. She quailed at the enormity of what lay ahead of her if she agreed.

She looked over at the curtained windows. Out there was everything she loved. The wild outdoors, the horses, the children who came to her for help, and the people who mattered most to her before Henri came into her life.

And there was her answer!

Before Henri came into her life.

Hadn't she already set arrangements in hand to distance herself from the farm and all the memories of Henri if he'd left without her?

The holiday to Australia.

After all, she couldn't get any further away from him or home than by retreating to the other side of the world. Whether she ever intended to return, she refused to admit, even while sitting on Henri's lap now.

"What would happen if your people found out about my healing abilities?"

"Not a thing," Henri assured her. "There are certain European countries that would frown on your gifts, but in your position you'd be able to work with them if you wanted to."

She heard the concern in his voice. "It's not a matter of wanting to," she said. "Sometimes, like the night you mentioned, it happens spontaneously."

"Then we will deal with it," he said. "Together."

Knowing she could handle everything else as long as she had Henri at her side, she slid her arms 'round his neck and kissed him. A long lingering kiss, full of promises, hopes, and dreams.

"If you had nothing, I would take you willingly—" She placed her fingers over his mouth before he could speak. "In many ways, it would be easier. I love you, Henri." She kissed him lightly on the lips, once. "You!" She traced her fingers over his lips, her eyes turning serious. "Only you," she said again, and brought her lips down on his in demonstration, before allowing an inch of space to develop between them.

"Who you are, what you are, is part of the package, the measure of my love, and yet my love cannot be measured. It is infinite, Henri. Without you, I am nothing. Oh, yes—" Again she stopped him from interrupting. "I would survive; I would live, but not fully. Never fully, if you are not at my side. I understand in my new life with you I will find many things difficult. But I would find life without you impossible to bear.

"I love you, Henri. I can't give you my heart, for you've had that from the moment we danced together at the palace. All I can give you is myself."

Henri lifted her off his lap and dropped to his knees.

"The life I live is not an easy one, and without you would become unbearable. The people around us will have their own agendas, some of which may conflict with our own. Knowing you has healed my heart. Before you, duty reigned, and obligation; after you, compassion. A wider understanding and love took precedence in my life, and with you I become a whole man. One who, with you at my side, will follow in my father's footsteps with the confidence that you will always be there for me in bad times and the good.

"When our people understand how you have healed me, they will open their hearts to you and everything you are. Before I came here, I told my father that unlike Liam, I would marry for convenience. For a fraction of a second I thought my comment disappointed him; now I see why. You are my chosen bride, Monica. You are the woman who has my heart in her hands. You are the woman I cannot live without. I love you.

"Will you marry me?"

"I will," she said, and dropped to her knees beside him.

Where, she wondered, had the golden heart pinned to the top of Henri's curtain come from, and who on earth had put it there?

Why had she even wondered when she knew there was more to heaven and earth than met the eye? Especially on Valentine's Day!

An hour later, with their hands linked, Monica and Henri made their way across the still-crowded dance floor to where Liam and Melanie sat.

"Where are the Terrible Twins?" Henri asked, unable to hide his grin.

"Working their way through every unattached female in the room," Melanie said with a laugh. "And where, might I ask, have you two been?"

"Talking."

Monica nearly choked at Henri's response.

"That must have been some talk. I hope you came to some positive conclusions," Melanie said.

"We did." Henri pushed Monica's left hand under Melanie's nose.

Her shriek almost paralysed everyone in the room.

The musicians bobbled their instruments and the women clapped their hands over their ears when the microphones clattered, banged, and whistled.

"Well, that's one way of gaining everyone's attention," Liam stated dryly.

Through a haze of joy, Monica watched the twins race across the dance floor, their partners forgotten.

"What?" Simeon's eyes narrowed when he took in the smiling faces in front of him. "What was all that caterwauling about?"

"Dash it, Melanie, did you have to scream like that? It's taken ten years off my life and what do I find when I get here? A bunch of Cheshire cats, that's what!" Sacha grumbled.

Behind them their guests stood transfixed as Liam crossed to the stage, dragging Henri and Monica with him.

"Ladies and gentlemen," he said. "On this most appropriate of days, Valentine's Day, it is my great pleasure to announce the betrothal of your friend and mentor, Monica, to my eldest brother, Henri Pierre Gasquet."

A roar went up, followed by a storm of clapping.

"A dance," someone shouted.

Liam leaned over to speak to the band leader, who shuffled his papers, talked to the other musicians, and waited for Monica and Henri to take to the floor.

"Oh!" Monica laughed and let her prince lead her into a waltz. "Henri, listen. They're playing Save the Last Dance for Me."

The End

About the Author

Sherry Gloag, a multi published author and member of the Romantic Novelists Association (UK), is a transplanted Scot now living in the beautiful coastal countryside of Norfolk, England. She considers the surrounding countryside an extension of her own garden, to which she escapes when she needs "thinking time" and solitude to work out the plots for her next novel. While out walking, she enjoys talking to her characters, as long as no other walkers are close by.

Apart from writing, Ms. Gloag enjoys gardening, walking, and reading. She also finds crystal craftwork therapeutic, and cheerfully admits books tend to take over most of the shelf and floor space in her workroom-cum-office.

Visit Sherry at http://www.sherrygloag.com. She loves to hear from her readers.

Also by Sherry Gloag

The Gasquet Princes
From Now Until Forever
His Chosen Bride

contemporary romances
The Brat
The Wrong Target
Duty Calls
He's My Husky
Name the Day
Ring of Truth

Regency romances
Honor's Dilemma
Vidal's Honor
No Job for a Woman

anthologies
The Magpie Chronicles
Nine Ladies Dancing

Thanks for reading! Dingbat Publishing strives to bring you quality entertainment that doesn't take itself too seriously. I mean honestly, with a name like that, our books have to be good or we're going to be laughed at. Or maybe both.

If you enjoyed this book, the best thing you can do is buy a million more copies and give them to all your friends… erm, leave a review on the readers' website of your preference. All authors love feedback and we take reviews from readers like you seriously.

Oh, and c'mon over to our website:
www.DingbatPublishing.ninja

Who knows what other books you'll find there?

Cheers,

Gunnar Grey,
publisher, author, and Chief Dingbat